Young Writers of Kern Anthology
2018–2019

Young Writers of Kern Anthology 2018–2019

WOK Press

ISBN: 0-578-50021-3

ISBN-13: 978-0-578-50021-8

Contents

2018

2019

2018

College

Anna Rocha Hart

California State University, Bakersfield

Anna Hart is a senior at California state University, Bakersfield. She is currently working towards completing her degree in Philosophy and feels that reading the work of past philosophers is what has given her a passion for defending free speech on college campuses. Upon graduation, Anna hopes to go on to earn her teaching credential so that she can provide future high school students with a classroom environment that fosters a diverse array of beliefs and opinions.

A few semesters ago, I heard a fellow classmate voice their opinion on the topic of free speech. This student claimed that the main duty of college campuses is to keep the students safe, and that in order to uphold this duty, speech on campuses must be restricted. I appreciated my classmate's opinion, but I disagree on these grounds: The main duty of universities is not strictly to keep students safe, but to provide them with a rigorous educational experience. This being said, the process of education itself is not inherently pleasant or pain free. The discovery of countervailing opinions through education which contradict all one had previously been taught to believe is likely to cause a deeply painful crisis. The beauty of education is that it forces us to reflect upon completely alien ideas, thereby forcing us to sort out our own thoughts and grow as human beings in the process. The loss of deeper knowledge and understanding that would be inflicted upon students should speech on campuses be hindered is ultimately a more devastating blow to the human experience than the damage which some suggest would be caused by allowing such speech.

Plato's "Allegory of the Cave" illustrates perfectly the uncomfortable aspect of education. Plato describes a person being forced out of the cave of ignorance, and into the sunlight of truth and knowledge, with the following example: "… Suppose … that he [the uneducated person] is reluctantly dragged up a steep and rugged ascent, and held fast until he's forced into the presence of the sun himself, is he not likely to be pained and irritated? When he approaches the light his eyes will be dazzled, and he will not be able to see anything at all of what are now called realities." (The Allegory of the Cave, Plato). If students attend university expecting to be safe from any emotional distress, then they are mistaken about the very nature of education. Allowing for many worldviews to exist on one campus facilitates the best possible learning environment, despite the discomfort that it is likely to cause when opposing worldviews collide.

In the wake of student protests against various speakers on campuses across America, it is not unusual to see images of raucous mobs of young men and women holding banners proclaiming, "Hate speech is NOT free speech." A CNN news article described a scene from one such protest- turned-violent at the University of Auburn, where white nationalist Richard Spencer was expected to speak. The article reports the incident that took place before the speech even began, "Students encircling the brawl said a Spencer supporter began jawing with an antifa, or anti-fascist, protester over Spencer's right to speak. A punch was thrown. The men spun through the crowd, swinging fists and grasping for headlocks before thudding to the ground," (War on Campus: The Escalating Battle Over College Free Speech, CNN). Understandably, these scenarios cause great concern for University administration and students alike, and it is reasonable for campuses to seek preventative measures against physical harm to students and faculty. The specifics of this prevention is up to each campus to determine. Disallowing controversial speakers, however, is not the solution. Where the problem arises is when universities begin to treat mere words as violence before physical violence has ever taken place. Some campuses have perhaps unintentionally perpetuated the idea that any view with which students strongly disagree is an inherently dangerous view, and students are ill-equipped to handle any such disagreement. Multiple protests illustrate that the violence is not caused by the words of the speaker, but by disagreements over whether that speaker should have the freedom to voice his or her opinion in the first place! A 2016 Gallup poll published this statistic: 54% [of students] say that the climate on their campus prevents some people from saying what they believe because others might find it offensive (Free Expression on Campus: A Survey of U.S. College Students, Gallup Poll). This is not a sentiment that should be shared by over half of the university student body in America. College campuses should be a bastion for the exchange of ideas and beliefs; instead, students either keep quiet for fear of merely offending another classmate or come to blows once they have been offended.

Every individual must be allowed to hear and share controversial views and have the autonomy to then decide for themselves which views are the correct ones. As the philosopher John Stuart Mill asserts, "The steady habit of [a person] correcting and completing his own opinion by collating it with those of others…is the only stable foundation for a just reliance upon it… knowing he has sought for objections and difficulties instead of avoiding them." Imagine a person born into a deeply racist environment where any speech denouncing racism is immediately quelled. All this person ever heard from their family and community around them is that certain groups are inferior due to the color of their skin. If that person never has the opportunity to question such a view by searching out opposing ideas which may initially be shockingly offensive, they will forever be stuck in that false mindset. Of course it can be argued that simply hearing opposing views will not change the racist's mind at all, and perhaps even solidify their prejudice, but that they have had the ability to challenge such views on their own is what is most important. The racist who is perpetually shielded from hearing the shocking claim that people of color are absolutely equal to him will never have even the chance to see personal progress.

Throughout my college career, I've heard professors, other students, and guest speakers flippantly make remarks that attacked some of my core beliefs. These experiences were certainly uncomfortable, but they never failed to provide valuable lessons. Without such discomfort, I would not have so closely examined my own views, and I am thankful that these men and women were able to freely share their views. Some of my beliefs have changed, and some have remained the same, but I am confident that I have not entrapped myself in a bubble of my own opinion. Of course it is my personal desire that people are civil with one another, but I would rather face great offense than risk the destruction of my own educational growth by limiting myself to only those opinions with which I agree. By banning certain speakers from campuses and censoring the kind of information that students are hearing so as to provide them with a "safe learning environment," universities are only doing their students a disservice. Students cannot learn when they are shielded from differing views, nor will they be equipped with the ability to know that their own views are worth holding.

Works Cited

Gallup, Freedom of Expression: A Survey of U.S. College Students and U.S. Adults. 2016. https://www.knightfoundation.org/media/uploads/publication_pdfs/FreeSpeech_campus.pdf

McLaughlin, Elliot C. "War on Campus: The Escalating Battle Over College Free Speech." CNN https://www.cnn.com/2017/04/20/us/campus-free-speech-trnd/index.html.

Mill, John Stuart. "On Freedom of Though and Expression." In Adams, David M. Philosophical Problems in the Law, by David M. Adams, 246. Boston: Wadsworth Cengage Learning, 2013.

Plato. Allegory of the Cave. Translated by Benjamin Jowett. Los Angeles: Enhanced Media, 2017.

Freedom of Speech in Public Universities

Kimberly Hernandez
California State University, Bakerfield

Kimberly Hernandez is a substitute teacher for the Bakersfield City School District. She is currently a senior at California State University Bakersfield and is expected to graduate in fall of 2018. Hernandez is pursuing a BA with a major in English and minor in Communications. She is passionate about writing and teaching. Hernandez's long-term goal is to become an educator and earn a platform through which she can share the importance of writing, and the significance of knowledge.

    The constitutional rights and freedoms granted to citizens of the United States are essential constituents of a nation that is habitually referred to as the "land of the free." Louis D. Brandeis, a Justice during a renowned court case involving Freedom of Speech, best described the significance of speech rights delineated in the First Amendment when he characterized free speech as an indispensable, and fundamental principle of the American government (Notable First Amendment Court Cases). Thus, when a constitutional freedom, such as Freedom of Speech, is remotely threatened, disapproval and protest can ensue. The issue of limitations on free speech is one that has persisted from the twentieth century to the twenty-first century. Public colleges and universities have particularly been at the center of the free speech debate. The implementation of speech codes, restrictions on public speakers, and lack of free speech zones have raised an argument on whether free speech interference from public colleges and universities is appropriate. A cogent argument against colleges and universities prying students' speech rights is that higher learning institutions should be free speech areas in which differences of opinions are welcomed. Yet, many public higher learning institutions continue to limit speech on campus as a claim to ensure student safety. The question arises - When is it appropriate for public higher learning institutions to restrict free speech? Or, is it appropriate to restrict speech at all? Although it is important for public colleges and universities to be proponents of diverse thinking and distinctive learning, limits to free speech in such institutions become necessary when speech incites violence or promotes an unhealthy environment for a person or group.

Resistance against free speech limits in public college and university campuses derives from the requisite that higher learning institutions should be places that encourage diverse, and sometime, even controversial thoughts. Rather than discourage notions that differ from the student population, higher learning institutions should be the place where students expand their knowledge on vast points of views. A stand against free speech limitations on public university campuses was illustrated in the case of DeJohn v. Temple University; during this case, Christian M. DeJohn defended his free speech rights after he commented on the ability of women to serve in combat and military forces (FindLaw). DeJohn felt that the Temple University's Student Code of Conduct, which banned sexual harassment, was an impediment on his ability to exercise his First Amendment rights to free speech (FindLaw). In this case, the court ruled in favor of DeJohn therefore supporting DeJohn's argument that the public campus' policies were infringing the civil freedom of expression.

The ruling on DeJohn v. Temple University exemplifies how, although some speech made on public institutions of higher learning may be offensive to those that disagree, unique speech is a right deserved by students. The ability for students to express different thoughts can result in intellectual stimulation of a public college or university campus. An article from Cornell University on speech rights perfectly illustrates how students have the right to expressive freedom of speech so long as the speech is "truthful or based on honest opinions" ("First Amendment). Permitting students to express thoughts that are divergent from one another is an essential right that should not be limited unless, there is a substantial basis of harm involved.

Recent cancellation of public figure visits to public colleges and universities, as well as implementation of speech codes, is reported by many campuses to be a safeguard for students. In an article titled Free Speech in the College Community, author Robert O'Neil elaborates on the proposition of speech codes. Speech codes at public universities and colleges establish guidelines to free speech which many students might interpret as restrictive. Despite the objection from some students, public institutions of higher learning continue to restrain free speech on campus. In recent events, speakers like Milo Yiannopoulos and Ann Coulter, have been prohibited or cancelled from speaking on certain public college and university campuses; these cancellations have been justified attempts by college campuses to ensure the safety of students.

In September of 2017, student members of California State University Bakersfield's political group, College Republicans, filed a statement against the university following the cancellation of a visit by public figure, Milo Yiannopoulos (Burger). In a statement titled, "Taking Back our University," the group of College Republicans exercised their first amendment rights by addressing a scheduled visit from controversial commentator, Milo Yiannopoulos. The statement was followed by outrage from the university group when CSUB requested that the event be either free to the public community or charged to students. The College Republicans were therefore unable to pay Yiannopoulos' speaking fees and they continued to claim that CSUB had intentionally restricted the group's freedom of speech. Although CSUB asserted that they advocated for free speech on campus, a concern with having Milo Yiannopoulos visit the campus would not be unwarranted or unjustified.

Subsequent to the disarray that was caused on UC Berkeley's campus due to a scheduled visit from Yiannopoulos, Ann Coulter, another controversial public figure, also had her visit to Auburn University cancelled (Ojavlo). Yiannopoulos was scheduled to appear on Berkeley's campus in February 2017; prior to his visit, a group of students who were opposed to having such a controversial speaker on campus, engaged in a protest that turned violent. The group of protestors resorted to threatening measures when they began vandalizing school property and throwing fireworks aimed at Berkeley police officers (Kim, Lilian, Laura). The ordeal was astonishing as UC Berkeley is home to one of the earliest efforts towards free speech. The Free Speech Movement of 1964 (Kim, Lilian, Laura). Decades after being home to the Free Speech Movement, Berkeley found itself under stringent speech control when it cancelled the scheduled visit from Yiannopoulos in February 2017. The cancellation of the university's free speech event is an example of a higher learning institution limiting free speech in an effort to keep students safe. Other campuses, like CSUB and Auburn University have now taken just safety measures by preventing speakers like Yiannopoulos since the presence of such speakers rouses the possibility of violence.

Despite objection against public colleges and universities limiting free speech on campus, recent studies show that restrictions are necessary under certain conditions. In a study conducted by UCLA professor, John Villasenor, students were questioned on whether it was acceptable to combat points of view that they disagreed with by using violence. Villasenor surveyed over a thousand students from over 49 distinct states; he found that the majority of students believed violence was an acceptable rebuttal when disagreeing with an opinion (Villasenor). The reaction from higher learning institutions to prevent this sort of violence is accompanied by an effort to reduce racism and harassment on campuses. Past court cases like Beauharnais v. Illinois, are demonstration that in cases where free speech incites hatred or violence on another person or group, limitation on speech is necessary (Sellars). Furthermore, public University of Wisconsin Madison gathered data that demonstrated positive effects on campus following implementation of stricter speech rules (O'Neil). After emplacing a speech code, University of Wisconsin reported "improvement in racial climate" (O'Neil).

Conclusively, intellectual stimulation and difference of opinions are essential for a flourishing public higher learning institution. However, different ideas and opinions should be, in the least, tolerated by opposing sides without resorting to threat or violence. When a person or group's well-being is compromised, speech codes and limits from higher learning institutions are entailed. Public higher learning institutions must be cautious when developing codes or limitations on campus. Students reserve the right to express themselves freely, disagree freely, and debate freely; college and university campuses offer areas where students can practice such freedoms, but these campuses must also be kept safe environments in which students can thrive.

Works Cited

Burger, James. "Cal State Bakersfield College Republicans Issues Statement on Milo Yiannopoulos' Visit." The Bakersfield Californian. The Bakersfield Californian, 25 Sept. 2017 www.bakersfield.com/new/cal-state-bakersfield-college-republicans-issues-statement-on-milo-yiannopolous/article_2ed6d630-a254-11e7-9bbd-a782f29ddb80.

"College Republicans Statement. pdf" The Bakersfield Californian, 25 Sept. 2017, www.bakersfield.com/collge-republicans-statement-pdf/pdf 587ce450-a256-11e-b82c-2367bdla87c6.html.html.

Equal Educational Opportunity and Free Speech on Public and University Campuses in California. California Advisory Committee to the United States Commission on Civil Rights. Oct. 2012.

"FindLaw's United States Third Circuit Case and Opinions: DeJohn v. Temple University." FindLaw: For Legal Professionals, Thomson Reuters, "First Amendment." LII/ Legal Information Institute, Cornell University, 6 Aug. 2007, www.law.cornell.edu/wex/firstamendmentcaselaw.find.law.com/us-circuit/1478578.html.

Kim, Lilian, and Laura Anthony, "Violent Protests over Yiannopoulos." ABC News, 1 Feb. 2017, abc7news.com/news/violent-protests-over-yiannopoulos-event-bring-chaos-to-berkeley /1732466/.

Ojavlo, Holly Epstein. "Do Controversial Figures Have a Right to Speak at Public Universities?" USA Today, Gannett Satellite Information Network, 21 Apr. 2017, College.usatoday.com/2017/04/20/do-controversial-figures-have-a-right-to-speak-at- public-universities/.

O'Neil, Robert M. Free Speech in the College Community. Indiana Press, 1997. EBSCOhost, Flacon.lib.csub.edu:2048/login?url=http://search.ebscohost/com/login.aspx?direct=true&db=nlebk&AN=23148&login.asp&site=ehost-live.

Rosenberg David, Racist Speech the First Amendment and Public Universities: Taking a Stand On Neutrality, 76 Cornell L. Rev. 549 (1991). Available at: http://scholarship.law.cornell.edu/clr/vol76/iss2/6.

Sellars, Andrew, Defining Hate Speech (December 1, 2016). Berkman Klein Center Research Publication No. 2016-20; Boston Univ. School of Law, Public Law Research Paper No. 16-48. Available at SSRN: https://ssrn.com/abstract=2882244.

Villasenor, John. "Views Among College Students Regarding the First Amendment: Results from a New Survey.." Brookings. The Brookings Institution, 18 Sept. 2017, www.brookings.edu/blog/fixgov.2017/09/18/ views-among-college-students-regarding-   the-first-amendment-results-from-a-new-survey/.

Freedom of Speech at Public Universities

Nicole Mirkazemi

California State University, Bakersfield

Nicole Mirkazemi is a current graduate of California State University, Bakersfield (CSUB) obtaining a Bachelor of Arts Degree in Political Science with a double concentration in Pre-Law and American Politics and a minor in Criminal Justice. She was nominated the 2018 Outstanding Student in Political Science and was inducted into the Roadrunner Society and Student Leadership Hall of Fame for both her academic achievements and leadership positions. Nicole has worked as a Research Assistant for one of her professors for almost three years and held multiple leadership positions at CSUB. Nicole is also one of two students who co-founded the Pre-Law Society at CSUB, providing students interested in law with events and opportunities to further their knowledge on law school and careers in law. Nicole is also a member of Pi Sigma Alpha: the National Political Science Honor Society, Alpha Chi: the National College Honor Society, and the Helen Louise Hawk Honors Program. Nicole is also a student scholar. She co-authored a chapter in Dr. Jeanine Kraybill's book: Unconventional, Partisan and Polarizing Rhetoric: How the 2016 Election Shaped the Way Candidates Strategize, Engage and Communicate. Nicole went on to have a paper published in the Spring 2018 Issue of Aletheia: Alpha Chi's Journal of Undergraduate Scholarship titled The Iran Nuclear Deal: The Influence of Congressional Speeches on Public Opinion.

Benjamin Franklin once asserted that "Freedom of speech is a principal pillar of a free government: When this support is taken away, the constitution of a free society is dissolved, and tyranny is erected on its ruins" (Shibley, 2016). As one of the freedoms our nation was founded upon, the freedom of speech was, and remains to be, an integral part of society. There are very few places that this freedom is so heavily employed than on college campuses. An unfortunate companion of the debate on free speech is the infringement on students' and professors' constitutional liberties. This can include, but is not limited to, free speech zones, limits on the guest speakers or panelists welcomed on campus, and flawed university policy. Of the top 409 schools in the United States, one in six hold restrictive free speech zones (Perrino, 2013). With universities striving to protect academic freedom, it is counterproductive to restrict the freedom of speech by students, faculty, staff, and/or guest speakers and panelists.

In 1964, students at the University of California, Berkeley started a movement, motivated and led by civil rights activists Jack Weinberg and Mario Savio, protesting bans on free speech. This later became known as the Free Speech Movement and has since led to a series of free speech debates. Protests, court cases, free speech zones, safe zones, and the media have propelled these debates forward. In 1988, the United States Supreme Court ruled on a case regarding the freedom of speech that would later be used in public universities to restrict student speech. In the decision of Hazelwood School District v. Kuhlmeier (1988), the court held that administrators can limit student speech, opening the door for schools to be overly restrictive (Hazelwood Sch. Dist. v. Kuhlmeier, 484 U.S. 260, 108 S. Ct. 562, 98 L. Ed. 2d 592 (1988)). In a 2002 U.S. Supreme Court opinion for Watchtower Bible and Tract Society of New York, Inc. v. Village of Stratton, Justice Stevens asserted that "It is offensive...in the context of everyday public discourse [that] a citizen must inform the government of her desire to speak...and then obtain a permit to do so" (Watchtower Bible & Tract Society of New York, Inc. v. Vill. of Stratton, 536 U.S. 150, 151, 122 S. Ct. 2080, 2082, 153 L. Ed. 2d 205 (2002)). The changing perspectives of the court on free speech have not helped resolve the issue. In the case of Stanley v. Georgia (1969), Thurgood Marshall, in the opinion of the court, asserted that the right to Freedom of Speech now includes the right to receive (Stanley v. Georgia, 394 U.S. 557, 569, 89 S. Ct. 1243, 1250, 22 L. Ed. 2d 542 (1969)). This is extremely important to take note of, especially in regards to the debates on college campuses involving guest speakers and panelists. If free speech includes the right to listen, then how are college campuses like the University of California, Berkeley, getting away with limiting this right (Park and Lah, 2017)?

The root nature of public universities should be to provide a place for discussion and debate on a wide range of issues. These institutions of higher learning have historically challenged the boundaries of society by encouraging diversity of thought and expansion of the human mind (Maloney, 2016). After all, these undergraduate institutions are usually the last time students are exposed to such a diverse set of opinions. Upon graduation, many individuals immerse themselves into their professions, surrounding themselves with likeminded individuals. One study found that individuals affiliate with others who are highly similar to themselves as a means of niche construction. In other words, it may be a hardwired trait within us to associate ourselves with those who are most similar to us (Bahns, Crandall, Gillath, and Preacher, 2017). Greg Lukianoff, First Amendment expert, and Jonathan Haidt, social psychologist, argue that three "Great Untruths," including the beliefs that one's feelings are always correct, that one should avoid any discomfort, and that one should only identify issues in others, are causing a great deal of harm to the current generation. This is essentially tearing college campuses apart. The protecting and coddling of the current generation is doing more harm than good (Lukianoff and Haidt, 2018). Universities today have made it quite clear that if students do not agree with another individual or feel uncomfortable by someone else's ideas, then that speech must be restricted or censored (Maloney, 2016). This is especially exemplified with guest speakers and controversial issues like abortion and religion. One key example is free speech zones. These are specific spaces or areas dedicated to free speech on college campuses. They essentially dictate where and when an individual can speak freely. One major concern regarding free speech zones is that the rest of the campus, a campus allegedly dedicated to stimulating debate, is now considered a restricted speech zone. This is just one avenue where administrators restrict speech. In the case of McGlone v. Bell, the Court of Appeals held that school policies requiring the disclosure of the content of speech was also an unconstitutional restriction on one's First Amendment rights (McGlone v. Bell, 681 F.3d 718 (6th Cir. 2012)), yet schools continue to monitor such speech, citing discomfort as a justification. Restrictions on speech out of this fear for discomfort has led to a reduction in the opportunities available to students. Guest speakers like Chris Rock and Jerry Seinfeld have written off college campuses as overly sensitive. But it doesn't stop there. Professors are now trained to avoid microaggressions, or words and phrases that have no initial malice but are seen as violent to certain groups, and to implement trigger warnings, or alerts that certain course curriculum may cause emotional distress (Lukianoff and Haidt, 2015). When it first emerged, I used to think the labeling of my generation as "Snowflakes" was completely unwarranted but I now see that it's becoming more and more of a realistic and well-suited name. This heightened goal to protect students from psychological harm is stunting our intellectual growth. Is it not the very goal of public universities to promote learning? It is essentially in the best nature of our students to be exposed to opposing, diverse speech. Diversity in intellectual outlook and cognitive style allows for an advanced community. Results from the National Study of Student Learning showed interactions and discussion with diverse peers fostered critical thinking among students (Fine and Handlesman, 2010). The creation of safe spaces to shield our students from uncomfortable discussions has created a culture where our future leaders think twice before they speak, fearing being charged with insensitivity (Lukianoff and Haidt, 2015). In the case of Sweezy v. New Hampshire (1957), Chief Justice Earl Warren emphasized that students and professors at universities must continue to freely question and speak. If this is no longer free throughout campus, society will stagnate (Sweezy v. State of N.H. by Wyman, 354 U.S. 234, 250, 77 S. Ct. 1203, 1212, 1 L. Ed. 2d 1311 (1957)). The very institutions that are tasked with preparing students for professional life are now doing quite the opposite with free speech zones, safe zones, and now the limiting of guest speakers.

Should public universities be able to restrict controversial guest speakers who do not align with and affirm the core values of the university in question? Or does the lack of validation promote the very same questioning that has led to major strides in U.S. history? The Socratic method, based on the idea that questioning beliefs stimulates critical thinking, leads to uncomfortable situations (Lukianoff and Haidt, 2015). Universities promote critical thinking in students as a major tool to propel them into the real world but then reverse this notion by limiting the very speech that could generate critical thinking through the restriction of guest speakers.

Speakers like Milo Yiannopoulos may appear to justify restrictions on free speech on college campuses as they are seen as lacking the capacity to intellectually stimulate students. However, as Thomas Jefferson argued, individuals in institutions should "not [be] afraid to follow truth wherever it may lead, nor to tolerate any error so long as reason is left free to combat it" (Lukianoff and Haidt, 2015). Rather than silencing those with whom we disagree, we should instead promote discussion to find truth as well as advance our values. Our Founding Fathers did not create the U.S. Constitution by restricting Great Britain's speech. Instead they created speech that is now the basis for our society. Abraham Lincoln did not combat slavery by restricting the Confederates' speech. Instead he delivered the Gettysburg Address and corrected invalid speech by having a louder voice. Martin Luther King, Jr.

did not lead the Civil Rights Movement by restricting discriminatory speech. Instead he spoke out against it with his famous "I have a dream" speech. Each of these public leaders have utilized speech to promote and advance their movements. Rather than restricting speech, institutions of higher learning should be promoting it.

Works Cited

Bahns, A. J., Crandall, C. S., Gillath, O., & Preacher, K. J. (2017). Similarity in Relationships as Niche Construction: Choice, Stability, and Influence Within Dyads in a Free Choice Environment. Journal Of Personality & Social Psychology, 112(2), 329-355. doi: 10.1037/pspp0000088.

Cohen, R. (2015). Teaching about the Berkeley Free Speech Movement. Social Education, 79(6), 301-308.

Fine, E. and Handlesman, J. (2010). Benefits and Challenges of Diversity in Academic Settings [Brochure]. Retrieved February 21, 2018, from https://wiseli.engr.wisc.edu/ docs/Benefits_Challenges.pdf.

Hazelwood Sch. Dist. v. Kuhlmeier, 484 U.S. 260, 108 S. Ct. 562, 98 L. Ed. 2d 592 (1988). Retrieved February 21, 2018, from https://1-next-westlaw-com.falcon.lib.csub.edu/ Lukianoff, G., & Haidt, J. (2018).

Coddling of the American mind: how good intentions and bad ideas are setting up a generation for... failure. Penguin Pr. Lukianoff, G., & Haidt, J. (2015, August 30). The Coddling of the American Mind. Retrieved March 04, 2018, from https://www.theatlantic.com/magazine/archive/2015/09/the-coddling-of-the-american-mind/399356/.

Maloney, C., Jr. (2016, October 13). College Campuses Have No Right to Limit Free Speech. Retrieved February 23, 2018, from http://time.com/4530197/college-free-speech-zone/

McGlone v. Bell, 681 F.3d 718 (6th Cir. 2012). Retrieved February 21, 2018 from https://1- next-westlaw-com.falcon.lib.csub.edu/.

Park, M., & Lah, K. (2017, February 02). Berkeley protests of Yiannopoulos caused $100,000 in damage. Retrieved February 22, 2018, from https://www.cnn.com/2017/02/01/us/milo-yiannopoulos-berkeley/index.html.

Perrino, N. (2013, September 13). How One College Student Fought His School's 'Free Speech Zone' - And Won. Retrieved February 21, 2018, from https://www.forbes.com/ sites/realspin/2013/09/13/how-one-college-student-fought-his-schools-free-speech- zone-and-won/#7ad7086b7e49.

Shibley, R. (2016, July 04). For the Fourth: Ben Franklin on Freedom of Speech-50 Years Before the Constitution. Retrieved February 20, 2018, from https://www.thefire.org/for-the-fourth-ben-franklin-on-freedom-of-speech-50-years-before-the-constitution/.

Stanley v. Georgia, 394 U.S. 557, 569, 89 S. Ct. 1243, 1250, 22 L. Ed. 2d 542

(1969). Retrieved February 21, 2018, from https://1-next-westlaw-com. falcon.lib.csub.edu/.

Sweezy v. State of N.H. by Wyman, 354 U.S. 234, 250, 77 S. Ct. 1203, 1212, 1 L. Ed. 2d 1311 (1957). Retrieved February 21, 2018 from https://1-next-westlaw- com.falcon.lib.csub.edu/.

Watchtower Bible & Tract Society of New York, Inc. v. Vill. of Stratton, 536 U.S. 150, 151, 122 S. Ct. 2080, 2082, 153 L. Ed. 2d 205 (2002). Retrieved February 21, 2018 from https://1- next-westlaw-com.falcon.lib.csub.edu/.

High School

Aaron Almaguer
Frontier High School

Growing up in Ventura County, Aaron Almaguer moved to Bakersfield in 2014. He was active in Scouts for many years. There he grew his relationships with fellow peers and leaders, learning about the importance of responsibility and integrity. He enjoys being outdoors, engaging in a wide variety of activities, such as kayaking and backpacking. His freshman year of High School, he joined the Frontier Swim Team. He is active in the school's Interact Club, Spanish Honors Society and enjoyed his first term on Prom Committee. If Aaron is not busy with volunteering, or outdoor activities, you can find him reading novels and books on philosophy.

☙

The commonality and relations between all humans is what unifies people and establishes the societies that represent certain groups' shared interests and goals. It is the obligation of individuals who represent a larger aggregate or community to assist in promoting and upholding the ethical code of their community as well as contribute to its growth and the well-being of other individuals in said community. In America, the ideals of "life, liberty, and the pursuit of happiness" are the tenets revered and upheld in this nation. It is the social responsibility of each American citizen to advocate and pursue these virtues in order to further the development of society and the individuals within.

Socially responsible Americans assist the growth of their community by volunteering and participating in other forms of philanthropy. Volunteering in churches, government, or charities elevate the standard of living for others in the community and creates more opportunities to pursue one's goals. Jennifer Self in her article, "Civic Responsibility", defines citizenship and social responsibility as "labors of ordinary people who created goods and undertook projects to benefit the public." It is considered the norm to contribute to the community in any possible way, rather than indulging in personal desires and activities that are only beneficial to oneself. For example, the youth organization, Boy Scouts of America, requires adolescents aspiring to earn their Eagle Badge, the organization's highest honor, to develop and lead a substantial service project in their community. These projects seek to improve their community for all individuals a part of it and show that the adolescents are capable of being productive and valued members of society. The duty of the individual is to contribute benefactions to their locality, hence their community may benefit from their alms.

The second central axiom of social responsibility is the promotion of morality. The morality of the community must be supported and represented by each person within the community in furtherance of sustaining the integrity of society. The Pachamama Alliance explains in their article, "Social Responsibility and Ethics," that in a larger scope, when a code of ethics is present, interactions with other groups and individuals also incorporates these elements of civic responsibility, as well as influences other assemblages of people. It is the public's social obligation to involve a code of ethics in everyday decisions to ensure not only their own moral growth, but also the growth of others with whom they come in contact with. The commonwealth of America has relied on one another since its inception. One such example of Americans upholding their code of ethics is the rescue group known as the Cajun Navy, who saved countless people during Hurricane Katrina and Hurricane Harvey when they assisted with the search and rescue of others in their community. These men used their skills and boats, motivated by their integrity and care of others in their community, to have a positive impact on their community during a time of crisis. One should strive to uphold their social responsibility and act on their conscience for the benefit of society.

There are however other people who would contend with this particular definition of social responsibility, arguing that volunteering or actively involving oneself in bettering the community is not necessary for social responsibility . Many argue that while volunteer work is beneficial to one's self and their community, it is not an obligatory activity in society, and therefore should not be considered the responsibility of each individual. Roselyn Polk, in her article "Social Responsibility," explains that "When we offer adolescents' participatory experiences that are meaningful, we allow them to discover their potency, ... and commit to a moral-ethical ideology." Volunteering not only aids adolescents with their transition into adulthood, it can also be a useful tool to help people of all ages contribute to society and help themselves grow. In a similar vein, if one views philanthropic acts as separate from the social responsibilities of a citizen, then they are essentially supporting the bystander effect, or the diffusion of responsibility within a group or other large capacity. This condition will ultimately leave the community to stagnate or even regress, damaging all those within it because of their belief that their neighbor would assist the community instead. Furthermore, the American society will not be able to evolve and develop without the contributions of the commonwealth, which makes it the responsibility of the masses to volunteer and add value to their community.

Civil obligations of the individuals in a community focus on beneficial gains and the betterment of the people included in it. Benefactions such as volunteering or donations improve both individual lives and that of the society. It is imperative that one also holds true to the core values of their society, in this case the American society, in favor of promoting these ideals and making them universal in the community.

Works Cited

Pachamama Alliance. "Social Responsibility and Ethics." Social Justice. Pachamama Alliance, N.d. Web. 30 Jan. 2018.

Polk, Roselyn K. "Social Responsibility." Evaluating the National Outcomes. The University of Arizona, N.d. Web. 30 Jan. 2018.

Self, Jennifer. "Civic Responsibility". Learning to Give. Learning to Give. org, N.d. Web 30 Jan 2018.

Álvaro Chumpitaz
Frontier High School

Álvaro Sebastian Chumpitaz Lavalle was born on September 17, 2001 in Neuquen, Argentina. Álvaro is a top student at Grtontier taking rigorous AP and Honors courses. He is deeply involved in clubs around his school such as Red Cross, Link Crew, and French Honors Society; furthermore, he is actively a leader at this schools as Frontier's Commissioner of Academics. Álvaro credits his success to his mother, Maria Lavalle, who taught him to have courage and strength to pursue is dreams; his father, Dino Chumpitaz, who taught him the value of honest and hard work; his sister, Gabriela Chumpitaz, who taught him maturity in the face of adversity; and his teacher, Lara Winn, who taught him to have confidence and faith in his abilities.

∾

Since the beginning of this nation, social responsibility provided the foundation of American society, as presented in 1787 in these famous words, "We the people of the United States, in order to form a more perfect union, establish justice, insure domestic tranquility, provide for our common defense, promote the general welfare, and secure the blessings of liberty to ourselves and our posterity, do ordain and establish this Constitution for the United States." The ideal of social responsibility has held strong and true from the establishment of the United States to the Civil Rights movement. But what does it mean to be a socially responsible member of American society? It is one who fights for justice and contributes their efforts to the improvement of society no matter the constraints of time.

Fighting for justice, advocating for what's right, and trying to correct injustices is what makes one a socially responsible member of society. During the 1960s-1970s, grassroots organizations emerged to fight environmental pollution and college campus protest demonstrations rose (Self 3). Whether it was fighting for environmental rights or to end US intervention in Southeast Asia, ordinary citizens took upon themselves an initiative to correct injustices in not only their government but also the world. Their efforts in fighting for justice allowed for the improvement of American society as well as the global society by promoting environmental conscientious and raising awareness of the negative effects of the US's "no end in sight" campaign on global and American stability. The efforts of American citizens to right injustices are exemplified throughout history such as the women's movement, the abolition of slavery, the organization of migrant workers, etc. (Nanzer 5). Evidently, modern society would not be a reality had it not been for the work of socially responsible members of American society such as Susan B. Anthony, Elizabeth Cady Stanton, Martin Luther King Jr., Cesar Chavez, and Abraham Lincoln. Each of these names and countless others played an important role in American society by fighting against injustices in their time in an effort to help their fellow man. By fighting for what's right in their respective time periods, these men and women performed their social responsibilities and instituted a more modern and equal American society as well as global society.

Socially responsible members of society are individuals who play a role in their community in an effort to contribute to the prosperity of the global community. Through volunteerism, individuals improved knowledge of themselves, their role in the political world, and their voting activity in later years (Polk 1). By actively helping in their community in their adolescence, teenagers exhibit a more known awareness of their role in the community and the impact of their actions. The knowledge acquired from youth volunteering experience allows the individual to develop or improve their sense of social responsibility. Volunteering also allows one to strengthen their community as well as interacting with different people (Bakersfield City School District 7). One who volunteers exhibits social responsibility by attempting to improve their community meanwhile also discovering the role an individual can have on society itself. And the ability to interact with people from all walks of life allows people to gain appreciation of different cultures, customs, and traditions which creates tolerant members of society aware of both the multiple ethnic aspects of American society but also of the world.

Some may say, social responsibility must adhere to the present laws of its time; it should be constrained to the reigning political system. The judicial branch has served, since the beginning of the US, as the determinant of the constitutionality of laws (5). But time has revealed political systems cannot always be upheld for their morality; from Dred Scott v Sanford to Citizens United v FEC, the Supreme Court has violated the morality and justice of society and failed to adhere to the core principles of social responsibility.

During the ratification of the Constitution, Founding Father Thomas Jefferson advocated for the insertion of the Bill of Rights, a document which would validate the rights of the common people and prevent their violation from an oppressive regime (5). Yet again, people identified that the government should not restrict social responsibility because it can have the potential to impede or destroy the ideal. Laws and decisions made by our government always change, but the ideal of social responsibility has remained constant in the American heart since the beginning. To constrain social responsibility to government power is immoral, unjust, and un-American.

Although America has a rich history of socially responsible citizens, in recent years the populace has lost sense of that ideal. It seems today that the forces pulling us apart are stronger than those binding us together; they divide us based on political parties, race, creed, origin, sexual orientation, gender, and religion. But America faces a new choice, Americans can forget their responsibilities and who they are in society or they can forge a new hope and revitalize that integral aspect of duty in themselves. To progress, America must remember what it means to be socially responsible, to fight against the injustice of time and contribute to the strength of the global community.

Works Cited

"Making a Difference: How to Become and Remain Active in Your Community-A Guide To Volunteering" The Advisory Bulletin. Bakersfield City School District, N.d. Web. 30 Jan. 2018.

Nanzer, Pat. "Individual Rights and Community Responsibilities." Learning to Give. Learning to Give, N.d. Web. 30 Jan. 2018.

Polk, Roselyn K. "Social Responsibility" Evaluating the National Outcomes. The University of Arizona, N.d. Web. 30 Jan. 2018.

Self, Jennifer. "Civic Responsibility" Learning to Give. Learning to Give, N.d. Web. 30 Jan. 2018.

What Makes America Great

KC Javier
Frontier High School

Born in the Philippines, KC Javier moved to America at the age of three. As a child, she was always engaged in extracurricular activities, such as basketball and playing the guitar at church. Currently at Frontier High School as a junior, KC is the Publicity Officer of Interact Club and Vice President of History Club as well the Co-founder and President of Asian Heritage Club. In addition, she is a member of Spanish Honors Society, National Honors Society, Key Club, MEChA Club, and Culture, a dance crew. She continually pushes herself to reach her full potential by taking every rigorous AP and Honors class that her school offers. Her studious and sedulous character allows her to maintain a 4.5 GPA while balancing her extracurricular activities and her job as a cashier. Aspiring to become an occupational therapist, she is looking forward to the exciting future that awaits for her.

ॐ

As a soldier trains before entering a battle, an adolescent must also be mentally prepared, properly equipped, and eager to serve their country as they enter adulthood as productive citizens. By instilling social responsibility at a young age, America successfully maintains a society of productive citizens. Emphasizing ethical values, active participation, and a strong sense of community, social responsibility is an essential factor of American society that contributes to the nation's ability to efficiently function as a democracy.

Utilizing child rearing, parents and teachers inculcate a sense of duty and ethical values. Assigned chores and telling the truth are the initial opportunities for children to exercise responsibility and integrity at home. Allowing them to make "meaningful contributions" (Polk 1) by completing chores, they begin to understand that there are certain obligations that they have to fulfill as a member of the family as well as introducing the concept of consequences for making poor decisions, such as lying; it prepares them for fulfilling obligations of being an accountable and respectable citizen with moral standards. Sharing the task with parents to "produce responsible citizens" (Self 3), teachers also include core values and life skills in their curriculum by training them to return library books on time, uphold academic honesty, and cooperate with other students on group projects. Advocating social responsibility and ethics by parents and teachers generates a "successful transition from adolescence into adulthood" (Polk 1); with early practice, it naturally develops in their personality and work ethic, which promotes future healthy habits, such as punctuality to interviews and integrity at work.

As ethics prepare the road to adulthood, it also creates a strong sense of civic duty, motivating active participation within the community.

After a vigorous effort to earn independence from Britain, America successfully birthed a democratic nation. Without participation in political affairs, America reverts back into a nation of voiceless people, and without the participation in communal affairs, there would be a lack of patriotism—both foreign to American culture. Taking pride in American citizenship, individuals must actively participate in the government and community in order for a democracy to function. To "uphold certain democratic values" (Self 2), citizens do not take for granted their rights, especially minorities and women who have zealously fought and earned suffrage; their underlying cause is identical to the reason why America sought to break from Britain—to be represented. To have a voice in the political system and choose to be voiceless would be foolish; what would be the point of democracy if we the people decide to opt out of the process of decision making in our own country? People are the "core of American democracy" (Nanzer 7) so participation is necessary for the nation's development and prosperity; it shapes the government, society, and ultimately, the nation's future. Equally important, citizens must be involved in communal affairs in order to make a difference, improving the nation as a whole.

By implementing ethical values and active participation among citizens, powerful community ties are imminent byproducts. As community service, club organizations, and churches strengthen the community by connecting people together, it increases the inclination to help one another. Volunteering benefits the individual with the "feeling of fulfillment" (Bakersfield City School District 10); giving them a meaningful role in society, benefactors feel accomplished and useful when assisting the beneficiaries.

Volunteering and other activities that are for the common good and are driven by a "shared sense of purpose" (Nanzer 7) create a supportive atmosphere of inclusionary affinity, harmoniously bonding citizens together—poor and rich, young and old.

Although adults are mainly in charge of the community, the youth play a significant role in the nation's success.

Although young age usually represents immaturity and indolence, the youth prove themselves to be contributing members of society. There are arguably "insufficient opportunities" (Polk 1) for the youth to exercise fruitful practice of citizenship as they are preoccupied with school. However, school actually connects the students with the community through after school sports, community service clubs, and other extracurricular activities. Extracurricular activities expand the life and social skills of a student by propelling them to take responsibility for themselves, such as managing their time wisely. Commencing a "culture of personal responsibility" (Greczyn 6), the youth is molded by important pillars of civic responsibility that are incorporated in daily life at school, such as "cooperation, respect, and participation" (Nanzer 7); sports are perfect for the development of these qualities since sportsmanship and teamwork are vital components for victory. In a similar manner, community service clubs directly connect and impact the community as the members volunteer to serve their community, constructing valuable lessons for students—altruism and benevolence. Sports, community service, and other extracurricular activities provided at school furnishes each student with opportunities to develop character, expand skills, and practice responsibility while having enjoyable experiences. However, as cell phones tend to have a major influence over their lives, an increasing number of teenagers prefer to spend time inside the realm of social media than outside.

Many claim that the generation of the Digital Age is too busy looking down at their phones into an abyss of social media to care about society, but in actuality, social media provides a medium for the youth to participate in political, communal, and even worldly affairs. Some may perceive their excessive attention on social media as inactivity within the community, which means opportunities to exhibit proper citizenship are "overlooked for personal gain" (Pachamama Alliance 3) or laziness. A common misconception is that teenagers devote all their time to themselves, their phones, and their facade that they build online to impress others rather than utilizing their time to be productive citizens. Accusations of selfish behavior and parochial mindsets contradict the reality of social media—access to a steady flow of updated current events and the ability to communicate, interact, and connect with people within the community, nation, and globe. Within seconds, tragic stories, such as mass shootings at school, flood the internet and the youth never fail to lend a helping hand. Raising awareness is the first step to creating a movement or reaching social justice for the affected group of people; it allows fellow Americans to acknowledge the problem, encourage compassion, and initiate reform within the political, educational, or social system promoting "positivity on and offline" (Monterey County Office of Education 9). Social media provides a way for teenagers to actively participate while bearing the responsibility to be the voice of the voiceless as well as advocates of social justice and reform.

As the youth learn, practice, and live with civic responsibility, America does not worry about its future but eagerly waits for the brilliance of our future leaders. America is a temple of democracy, which means that a communal effort is required—making each person essential. As social responsibility—ethical values, active participation, and a strong sense of community—embody the societal mindset of our citizens, our nation continues to thrive with success, honor, and prestige.

Works Cited

Alliance, Pachamama. "Social Responsibility and Ethics." Pachamama Alliance. Pachamama Alliance, n.d. Web. n.d.

Greczyn, Robert. "Where the Buck Stops: Personal Responsibility in a 'Not Me' Society." Walker College of Business. Walker College of Business, 2015. Web. 30 Nov.   2015.

"Making a Difference: How to Become and Remain Active in Your Community-A Guide to Volunteering." Bakersfield City School District. Bakersfield City School District, n.d. Web. n.d.

Nanzer, Pat. "Individual Rights and Community Responsibilities." Learning to Give. Learning to Give, N.d. Web. 30 Jan. 2017.

Polk, Roselyn K. "Social Responsibility." Evaluating the National Outcomes. The University of Arizona, N.d. Web. 30 Jan. 2018.

"Responsible Use of Social Media." Monterey County Office of Education. Monterey County Office of Education, 2014. Web. 30 Jan. 2018.

Self, Jennifer. "Civic Responsibility." Learning to Give. Learning to Give, n.d. Web. n.d.

Social Responsibility in Modern America

Josh Lopez
Frontier High School

While writing has long been a passion of mine, music is Josh's true love. He has played the guitar since he was seven years old. He has enjoyed finding ways to use music to help others. His band has played charity concerts for local Rotaries and for veteran benefits. "It was incredibly rewarding to help people by doing something I love," says Josh.

Josh's desire to help people extends beyond his hobbies and into his career plans. He would like to study nuclear physics in order to develop a new source of sustainable energy. Creating a viable means to harness the power of fusion reactions would unlock the door for a greener future for posterity. He aspires to endow a lasting impact on the world. "After all," he says, "I was taught to always leave a locale in a better condition than I found it."

Imagine for a moment a city where nobody is left wanting for food or shelter, where there is no wage inequality, and without pollution. Imagine a city where there are no corporations making millions while they are barely paying their employees livable wages. This may seem like an utopia, yet there is only one thing that separates our cities from the imaginary: social responsibility. Here in Bakersfield, like many other cities all over the world, most citizens go about their daily lives without ever thinking about the big picture that is the community. For many, neither the thousand people who roam the streets at night without a home, nor the 26.7% of the population who are living below the poverty line ever cross their mind. When citizens consider the needs of the whole community and contribute to the common good, social issues such as homelessness, hunger, and civil rights infringements are minimized. Civil responsibility is the culmination of community activism, a big picture mindset, and social awareness.

Community activism has had a profound effect on society. When large groups work together to right wrongdoings in their communities, they are seldom defeated. "Voluntary actions by private citizens working together to right injustices, change directions, and pursue benefits for the common good are noted throughout American history. This list includes the abolition of slavery, women's suffrage, public education, community hospitals, the civil rights movement, the environmental movement, and the organization of migrant workers" (Nanzer 2). In each of these examples, injustices have been abolished through the coordinated efforts of citizens who are dissatisfied with an unjust law or the present conditions of their communities. It is of the utmost importance for all citizens to remain involved in their communities in order to keep cities moral and ethical in their laws and business practices. In addition to bettering society, volunteerism can benefit upcoming generations. "When we offer adolescents participatory experiences that are meaningful, we allow them to discover their potency, assess their responsibility, acquire a sense of political process, and commit to a moral-ethical ideology." (Polk 1). By teaching the young the importance of community activism and volunteering, the future of Bakersfield becomes brighter than ever.

Another vital aspect of social responsibility is the ability to consider the wellbeing of the community as a whole. Nearly every act of social injustice occurs because people are so caught up in their own selfish needs that they do not know or care how it affects others. Social responsibility is founded upon the belief that "Every individual has a responsibility to act in a manner that is beneficial to society and not solely to the individual" (Social Responsibility and Ethics 1). An altruistic mindset is imperative to the betterment of any organization, for it requires people to put the needs of others above their own desire for leisure in order to inspire citizens to action. "Getting to a point where everyone does their part requires... a shift in a collective mindset that has developed because we have allowed an incredibly important trait to slowly leach out of our society's character. That trait is personal responsibility" (Greczyn 1). There are no big steps in creating a better community, for it is the result of lots of little steps from many different people. Social responsibility is the culmination of a large group of individuals with a strong sense of personal responsibility. A dedicated group effort is the only way to spur long term, lasting change in our society.

The final component of social responsibility is social awareness, for there is no way to conquer injustice if communities do not know about the transgressions. "It is the responsibility of the individual to watch over a community to make sure that standards are objective and beneficial to human life" (Nanzer 2). By remaining informed and involved in the affairs of a community, an individual is able to ferret any breaches in civil rights or social injustices so that they may begin the process to rectify them. It is important to remain up to date on current events in a community. Vigilantly checking reputable local news sources and paying attention to current events are two ways of remaining socially aware. If the problems in society are never elucidated, citizens besmirch the integrity of their communities.

A common excuse for eschewing community service is a scarcity of opportunities. It is argued that "there is an impression of emptiness in the role of today's youth due to insufficient opportunities for self-discovery through action, social contributions, and experimentation with various adult roles" (Polk 1). Aside from numerous programs at homeless shelters, animal shelters and other volunteer driven organizations, this is a fallacy because citizens do not need to be part of an organization to serve their community. Community service may take the form of picking up litter off of the street on daily walks, bringing food to a homeless person nearby, or countless other tasks. Therefore, arguing that there are not enough ways to help is just another way of extenuating and is a prime example of a philosophy which Robert Greczyn Jr., CEO of Blue Cross, calls "Not Me-ism" (Greczyn 2). Greczyn explains that not only does an increase in personal responsibility increase productivity, but it characterizes the individual "as a leader" (Greczyn 3). Here citizens are offered the choice to either be one of the many who practice "Not Me-ism" or to rise to the occasion and be an upstanding member of society.

Social activism, an altruistic point of view, and awareness are the three pillars on which social responsibility are built. When these practices are put to use by citizens, social injustice is minimized and communities are strengthened. While some may argue that there is a lack of service opportunities for youth, there are plenty of ways that young citizens can help their communities. Activism can take the form of volunteerism or standing up to social injustices. By taking personal responsibility for the wellbeing of the community, citizens demonstrate altruism. Community awareness can be worked into any daily routine by watching reputable news sources. In conjunction with one another, these practices bring communities closer to the aforementioned utopia with every citizen who practices them.

Works Cited

Polk, Roselyn K. "Social Responsibility." Evaluating the National Outcomes. The University of Arizona, D.d. Web. 30 Jan. 2018.

"Social Responsibility and Ethics." pachamama.org. Pachamama Alliance, N.d. Web. 16 Feb. 2018.

Self, Jennifer. "Civic Responsibility." learningtogive.org. Web. 16 Feb. 2018.

Graczyn, Robert Jr. "Where the Buck Stops: Personal Responsibility in a 'Not Me' Society" Business.appstate.edu. Blue Cross and Blue Shield of North Carolina, D.d. Web. 16 Feb 2018.

Nanzer, Pat. "Individual Rights and Community Responsibilities." Learning to Give. Learning to Give, N.d. Web. 30 Jan. 2017.

Being Socially Responsible in American Society

Nicholas Romasanta

Frontier High School

Nicholas Romasanta was born in Bakersfield California, his parents immigrants from the Philippines. Early on in life he picked up basketball and swimming, and played in the school band. As a student at Frontier, not much has changed. He still continues swimming and is a part of Frontier's varsity swim team. Nicholas is also currently the drum major of Frontier's marching band, and plays the bass clarinet for the wind symphony. He is also a member of the Interact Club, Asian Heritage Club, and National Honors Society. Outside of school, he frequently volunteers at Mercy Hospital.

America's history is one full of both social triumphs and cruel subjugations. One thing remains constant throughout its long history, however, and that is the courage of the people to protect its community. From the American Revolution to the Vietnam War, from women's suffrage to the Black Lives Matter movement, the American people will find some way to stand together for what they believe to be right. Standing together against injustice and wrongdoing has become an American tradition, and that sort of social justice has become the obligation bestowed upon every American. This idea of righteousness shapes the mindset of a socially responsible member of American society—the unselfish commitment and desire to work for, and safeguard, a sense of moral integrity and kindness in both the individual and the community.

The preservation of moral values and human rights is essential for any society to prosper. To not support these values or rights, with the intention to "...harm society or the environment... would be considered to be socially irresponsible" (www.pachamama.org). A sense of devotion to the community must then be profoundly strong in a socially responsible citizen, meaning that the community's needs cannot be harmed for the sake of personal interest. However, when these values are under danger, it is the duty of a citizen to take action, as "...the rights of the people are core of American democracy... its tradition of individual rights strongly reflects the American experience" (Nanzer 2). Even to this day, the protection of American ideas and freedom is as crucial as ever in the face of both foreign and domestic terrorism. Defending this noble tradition is every American's civic duty, as without it, the treasured concepts of equality and democracy would cease to exist.

Protecting a community does not have to be an individual effort. From its conception, a community is not the work of a single man or woman, as Jennifer Self claims, "From voluntary fire departments to the public arts to the Civilian Conservation Corps... citizens participated in projects that shaped communities and ultimately the nation" (www.learningtogive.org). Through teamwork, these people would be the ones who both created and defended their community. In every instance where society was protected from wrongdoing, there are "... people [who] voluntarily came together with a sense of purpose for the common good" (Nanzer 1). Without the determination of the people, there can be no community. A community lives and breathes through those within it, thus, without a sense of unity, a society can collapse.

Various communities in history have thrived under strong figures in leadership.

Martin Luther King Jr., Mary Wollstonecraft, and Cesar Chavez all helped to inspire hope in those who looked up to them. As Robert Graczyn Jr. proclaims in his speech, "...when everyone does their part, the sum of those individual efforts— with the right leadership—can have a lasting impact." With exceptional leadership comes organization and effectiveness, helping to drive progress forwards. For one to be a leader, however, Gracyzn Jr. also asserts that, "True leaders embrace the principle of personal responsibility themselves." These "true leaders" exhibit a strong personal integrity, which enable them to have a heartfelt dedication to society. There is nothing wrong with working with others or acting as an individual, however, leading the charge for the protection of the common good can reflect a strong sense of commitment and social responsibility.

There may be disagreement when it comes to how active someone should be in a community, where simply being kind to others and minding your own business is all that needs to be done to be socially responsible. As Graczyn

Jr. says in regards to this, he says, "It's easy to look around and wonder how just one person can have any effect." This is a looming concern for those not confident in their own ability to do a service to their community. To this, there is a solution: do not do it alone. For those still hesitant, perhaps because they are still not confident in themselves, Polk K. Roselyn claims that, "Adolescents learn social responsibility and social skills through interaction with their family, peers, mentors, and communities" (Evaluating the National Outcomes). Polk's claim supports the idea that people are influenced by those around them, and can draw valuable lessons from them. Therefore, by working with and looking to others for guidance, being an active, socially responsible citizen is a practical, doable task.

America's history is full of socially responsible citizens. The determination of those in the past leaves something for us today to look up to. Protecting the ethics of society and the rights of the people is a distinct part of American culture that will live on in the hearts of the its citizens for decades to come. By maintaining a steadfast devotion to the protection and practice of righteous morals and values, the true meaning of social responsibility can be found.

Work Cited

Graczyn, Robert. "Walker College of Business." Where the Buck Stops: Personal Responsibility in a "Not Me" Society, 30 Nov. 2015, business. appstate.edu/events/boyles-ceo-lecture-series/where-buck-stops-perso nal-responsibility-not-me-society.

Polk, Roselyn K. "Social Responsibility." Evaluating the National Outcomes. The University of Arizona, N.d. Web. 30 Jan. 2018.

Self, Jennifer. "Civic Responsibility." Civic Responsibility | Learning to Give, www.learningtogive.org/resources/civic-responsibility.

"Social Responsibility and Ethics | Who Is Responsible And Why?" Who Is Responsible And Why? | Pachamama Alliance, www.pachamama.org/ social-justice/social-responsibility-and-ethics.

Middle School

American Pride and Values

Gurnoor Bhatti
La Viña Middle School

Gurnoor Bhatti graduated from La Vina Middle School in the spring of 2018. With a love of writing from a young age, Gurnoor says writing brought joy and a chance to express emotions about current events she feels strongly about. Quoting favorite author Ann Rand, "Words are a lens to focus one's mind," Gurnoor completely agrees and is thankful for the opportunities presented to her to be able to write and share views with others who want to hear what Gurnoor has to say.

❧

"We cannot always build the future for our youth, but we can build our youth for the future," - Franklin Delano Roosevelt. As future generations develop, we must construct a certain set of expectations in order to keep the world from chaotic disaster. In America, how we act in society is a significant part of who we are as individuals. In society, Americans who perform their civic duties, present ethical behavior, and nurture the Earth for the future generation are deemed as socially responsible members of American society.

As a part of America, we have civic duties and responsibilities. Our citizenship binds us to the government to accomplish these tasks. Crucial duties that should be performed by us are obeying the law, actively participating in our community, and standing up against injustice. If we as citizens of America do not obey the laws set by our federal government, we are not socially responsible. Even by following the simplest of laws, such as stopping when there is a red light, can make a difference. For instance, let's say you have decided to run a red light. The car who has the right to turn turns, but your decision to run the red light causes a collision between the two cars, resulting in the death of the other individual. If you had done your civic duty and obeyed the law, you could have saved a life. Another American duty of ours is actively participating in our community. By participating, we can help resolve conflict that is occurring or rectify our community. In Delano, we have a community garden to provide space for urban gardeners who have no suitable space to grow fruits and vegetables. Our garden allows residents to grow their own produce to save money and live a healthier lifestyle. Locals who live near beaches get together and pick up waste to keep our oceans sanitary. Banding together as one united whole for one cause, even the smallest community can bring a positive change to the world. As civilized Americans, we must stand up and take action against injustice. Imagine sitting in your classroom and working on a project about one of the most impactful events in history: the September 11 attacks. You see a few students laughing at a drawing: a hijacked plane crashing into the Twin Towers and notice that in the drawing there is a picture of a smiling Sikh girl that is in your class pasted on the windows of the plane. One of the students says, "Oh no! There is a terrorist in the room!" This is the exact injustice that my sister went through. Throughout our school years, my sister and I have dealt with hurtful racism. Students called us terrorists and believed that we should not stay in this country. Though many belittled us, others stood up for us because as stated in our Pledge of Allegiance, "[there is] one Nation under God, indivisible, with liberty and justice for all." America believes in liberty and justice for every individual, but in order to achieve justice, we must stand up for those who are still constantly being hurt due to their color, race, or gender. Performing our civic duties demonstrates that we have priorities in our everyday lives.

Mostly, people interact with other individuals in public on a daily basis. When in a public setting, they need to provide ethical behavior. Ethical behavior means to act in such a way which society considers proper values. According to Pachamama.org, ethics "should be incorporated into daily actions/decisions, particularly ones that will have an effect on other persons and/or the environment." Ethical behavior also shows an individual's personality. Behaving in an ill-mannered way can show people that you are arrogant, while behaving in a helpful manner shows that you have social manners. Ethical behavior helps foster a positive environment for us and our surroundings.

For the future generations to come and enjoy our beloved Earth, it should be nurtured with eco-friendly decisions. Recently the Earth's health has been very poor due to the environmental issues at hand. An issue our Earth has been dealing with is fossil fuel emissions. Fossil fuels are a natural fuel such as coal or gas, formed in the geological past from the remains of living organisms. These fuels need to be reduced soon or our air will be polluted with more harmful toxins. There are a couple of ways to reduce fossil fuels such as changing your transportation, relying on sustainable energy, or using more fuel-efficient vehicles. Another problem that is affecting the Earth negatively is deforestation. Deforestation is the destruction of forests to make the land available for other uses. NASA believes that if the current deforestation levels proceed, in no more than 100 years, all of the rainforests in the world will be wiped out. Trees provide us with oxygen, and without a lasting supply of trees, there could be a sooner decline of the human civilization. The main causes of this harmful act are chopping down trees for fuel, making more available land for housing, and harvesting timber to create commercial items. In order to protect our trees to last longer, we should buy items that are mostly recycled, buy sustainable wood products, use less paper, and restore degraded forests. The lack of recycling is also a major problem in our ecosystem. Millions and millions of pieces of plastic get thrown in the ocean because too many people are not actively participating in more efficient choices for our Earth. Confused for food, the plastics get consumed by the marine animals. Humans eat these "contaminated" fish, not knowing there is plastic in the fish. If we begin to recycle consistently, we can have healthier food sources, pollution will be reduced, and there will be larger marine animal populations. The Earth will sustain its enjoyment only if we nurture it and take eco-friendly decisions.

Being a part of America means we should attempt to be model citizens and follow the values society deems are proper. We should bring progress to our nation, so not only it will benefit us, but the world as well. Without progression, there is no growth and without growth, our civilized country will not have the chance to thrive and prosper. Performing our civic duties, presenting ethical behavior, and nurturing the Earth is what it means to be a socially responsible member of American society.

Ways to Be a Socially Responsible Member of American Society

Darien Alexander Brandon
Lakeside School

Darien Brandon is a student from Lakeside School. Darien's hobbies include drawing, playing video games, and talking with friends. Darien's favorite animal is a llama because "they are better than any other animal." In his spare time, Darien plays Fortnite, and dies all the time.

"Every good citizen makes his country's honor his own, and cherishes it, not only as precious, but as sacred. He is willing to risk his life in its defense and is conscious that he gains protection while he gives it." This is a quote from Andrew Jackson, our 7th president, and he claims that a citizen should protect, love, and use their rights. He is telling us what to do and how to be socially responsible in American society which benefits and supports our country and our community. Working with nonprofits, helping people in your community, and fighting for good causes are great ways to be a socially responsible member of American society.

Being part of a nonprofit organization is a great way to be a socially responsible member of American society. United Way Worldwide is a nonprofit organization that works hard to have healthier and smarter people with profitable jobs. The people in this organization are wonderful examples of being a good citizen of the United States of America. They are trying to help the world even though they are not being paid for it. Another nonprofit organization working for an important cause is the American Cancer Society. It is trying to cure cancer and help everyone with it, and they are taking their time away voluntarily to help end cancer. The people in this organization are amazing citizens, and anyone can join it and be like them. Even though being part of a nonprofit organization makes you a socially responsible member in the United States of America, there are other ways to help people.

Helping people in the community shows that citizens are socially responsible members of American society. According to onefamily.com, one of the best ways to help people in the community is to donate to charities, homeless shelters, and animal shelters. Citizens will be helping the homeless people in their community and they will help support their local charities. This shows the community that they are caring and responsible. Another way to help the community is to clean up the local area. By picking up trash, they are making the community look nicer and cleaner. Also, they can recycle trash that they find on the ground which helps everyone. In these ways, citizens are being socially responsible in their own community and in America.

If citizens fight for good causes and for their rights, they are being strong and responsible members of American society. Martin Luther King Jr. was the leader of the Civil Rights movement which fought for Black rights in America. He succeeded, and he earned Black people more rights. If we act against injustices in our country as Martin Luther King Jr. did, we are helping our country and the people in it. Our own sixteenth president, Abraham Lincoln, is a great example of fighting for good causes. He ended slavery in America, and he led his soldiers into the Civil War to end it. By following his example, citizens can work hard to fight for what is right. Fighting for everyone's rights is an important way to be a socially responsible member of American society.

If citizens want to be socially responsible members of American society, they should work on nonprofits, take action in their community, and support good causes. First, nonprofits are trying to help people, and they should be a part of that. As a socially responsible member of American society, they should want to help people everywhere. Also, citizens in their community should help and donate to homeless shelters, animal shelters, and charities. Next, people who support and fight for good causes are being amazing citizens. As a citizen of the United States of America, they should be fixing things that are wrong in their community or even in their country. These are great ways to be socially responsible members of American society, and they are important to being a citizen of the United States of America.

Socially Responsible

Lorena Coronado
Lakeside School

At the time of her entry, Lorena Coronado was in the 7th grade at Lakeside Middle School. Some of her hobbies include reading, swimming, and hanging out with her family. Her high school goals are to improve her writing skills, graduate with an overall 4.0 GPA, and to make a career out of swimming.

Cesar Chavez once said, "We cannot seek achievement for ourselves and forget about progress and prosperity for our community…Our ambitions must be broad enough to include ambitions and needs of others, for their sake and for our own." Cesar Chavez, like many others, was passionate about changing something that was unfair. Society is the aggregate of people living together in a more or less ordered community. Anyone can contribute to the society by helping or volunteering in the community because if one person can make a difference, so can you. To become a socially responsible member of American society, you must be passionate, confident, and take action.

A quality that makes one a socially responsible member of an American society is being passionate because it shows strong belief in what one is standing up for or what they support. Someone who was passionate was Martin Luther King Jr. Doctor King fought for racial equality and the abolishment of the segregation of whites and blacks. He believed colored people needed to have the same rights as white people. On the website, Biography of Martin Luther King Jr, Martin Luther King Jr is quoted as saying, "I have a dream that my four little children will one day live in a nation where they will not be judged by the color of their skin but by the content of their character." He was passionate that one day African-American men, women, and children would not be judged by the color of their skin. Being passionate about what you support is important to American society.

Another quality that makes you a socially responsible member of American society is being confident. Meghan Markle, according to a video produced by A Plus, became a female advocate for women rights at age eleven. In the video it stated that she was in school watching a TV show and it showed a dishwashing liquid commercial. The tagline said, "Women all over America are fighting greasy pots and pans." Two boys, in her class, told her that is where women belong, in the kitchen. Megan felt sad and angry because that wasn't right. Her father encouraged her to write a letter to three people that made her believe: Hillary Clinton, Linda Ellerbee, and the dishwashing company because she wanted to change something that wasn't right. The commercial changed its approach from only targeting women to targeting everyone. She made an impact on American society by showing women are more than just a housewife. She showed qualities of being confident by actually doing something to change American society.

Finally, a quality that makes one a socially responsible member of American society is taking action. Winter Vinecki took action because she saw that there wasn't enough money for cancer research. Winter, at the age of twelve, started to raise money for cancer research. She wanted to take action because she wanted to make a difference for those suffering from cancer. Winter made an impact on American society by changing cancer patients' lives.

Being a socially responsible member of the American society is helping your community and volunteering. Some people are not being socially responsible members of American society. They are socially isolated, do not volunteer, and do not help out in the community. We, as a community, should help others. Whenever we help someone, we feel a joy of accomplishment and connection with other people. You can be inspired by volunteering in a place you love to go or that brings you joy.

When one considers being a socially responsible member in society, one must possess many qualities such as creativity, an outspoken voice and patience. When you are creative, you can come up with new and improved ideas to help your community. Being outspoken means being frank and stating one's opinion. Being patient will help you reach your goal to helping your community. You have to take action when helping. You can be a socially active member in your community by volunteering or standing up for something that you believe in.

What it Means to Be a Responsible Member of the American Society

Kaelyn Gray
Fruitvale Junior High School

Kaelyn is a 7th grader at Fruitvale Jr. High. Kaelyn is an excellent student. She enjoys art, playing volleyball, and writing, and enjoys spending time with her two dogs and six cats. Kaylen also has two sisters. She hopes to be known for someday writing a book that will have an impact on others.

∽

A responsible member of the American society can mean many things. To the older generations, it can mean work, family, and ethical behavior. Younger generations believe in education and societal roles. On the whole, most people will believe that being a productive member of the American society includes providing not only for ourselves but for future generations as well.

Today, younger members of society are dealing with a society very unlike that of their parents and grandparents. Environmental issues are on the forefront of many minds. Global warming and changing climates are leaving our world with issues that were not present ten to twenty years ago. This has a huge impact on what it means to grow up in the American society today. Recycling, finding ways to keep the air and climate clean, and reducing trash is a not just a community issue but a surmounting global issue. It is fair to say that most young people today believe their responsibility to society is to ensure that the planet remains habitable for future generations to come.

While older members of society may feel similar regarding the climate and environment, they have lived through many other issues. Most notably are the various wars in which have consumed our planet in the last couple of decades.

In this respect, being a responsible member of society encompasses more esoteric truths including citizenship, allegiance, and sense of duty. Therefore, it is equally important to care about the world we live in as well as take pride in the country we reside in.

Invariably, the ideals and beliefs of the older generations are passed down to the younger generations. Societal norms and roles are enforced across the nation in day-to-day interactions. Kids first learn about responsibility to society at home. As they grow and learn they come to realize that being socially responsible also means to be human. Social responsibility is not limited to caring for the environment or for one's country but ultimately it means caring for one another. This is the greatest legacy that is passed from generation to generation and is the defining characteristic of whether society continues to flourish or meets its demise. Compassion and empathy for one another is truly what it means to be a responsible member of any society. Without these two elements society itself would be meaningless.

Being a responsible member of the American society therefore means caring about the environment, allegiance, community, and compassion. When individuals care more about their friends, family and neighbors they are ensuring the very survival of society. It is the individual's duty to not only worry about the environment they live in, but ensure they are caring about who they share that environment with.

What Does It Mean to Be a Socially Responsible Member of American Society?

Bhargavi Gulia
Fruitvale Junior High School

Bhargavi Gulia is a seventh grade student in Fruitvale Junior High School. She lives in Bakersfield, California with her parents and younger brother. This twelve-year-old enjoys writing essays, stories, poems, and composing songs. She has been composing songs since she was six years old. Bhargavi also loves to do mathematics. She enjoys her free time playing UNO and badminton with her family and watching television. Bhargavi is a caring person who stands for her family and friends. Bhargavi looks forward to publishing her composed work!

જ

Social responsibility is a "...code of conduct and action beyond what is required by laws [and] regulations ...", as Laura Dragonette describes on Investopedia.com. It's a deed done by one who has a will to serve others without any expectations of personal benefit(s) or reward(s). Our society benefits from everyone's ethical conducts. But is social responsibility good or bad? Some don't want to interfere in others' lives while many want to help their community as much as possible. But what does it mean to be socially responsible? How can someone become socially responsible? Why should they participate if nothing tangible is received? Which types of attitudes should be displayed? What are some examples of civic responsibility? And what are some oppositions to good citizenship?

From my perspective, everyone should demonstrate social responsibility. People are helping others for the benefits of the person in need and for their community. It helps the society grow with the little steps taken. These littles steps slowly open doors to larger ideas. Everyone should do something beneficial for the American society.

To be socially responsible means to serve the community, voluntarily, to make its residents happier and healthier! Cram.com remarks that, "[Social responsibility is] taking an active participation in resolving some of the issues..." This means that solving current issues is being responsible. It's where people work together to come up with an answer. When asked "What is social responsibility?" on quora.com, Autumn Knudson answered, "... [it is the] responsibility to improve the world around them for the benefit of all." The necessity of the members of a community to improve their community is the definition of social responsibility. To be a responsible citizen means to help others for the benefit of the community.

There are a lot of ways to be socially responsible. The Citizen's Almanac: Fundamental Documents, Symbols, and Anthems of the United States says to "Stay informed of the issues affecting your community." The people should know what the issues in their community are. They are helping their community by being able to guide them with their knowledge. "Participate in your local community." Residents of a community could help a local hospital by giving the patients a visit. Similar services allow others to be happy. Laura Dragonette suggests to participate in the community by doing what amuses the person. When someone, "... [acts] in the best interests of their environments and society...", it allows them to serve others with a smile on their face. The happier someone is in what they are doing, the more effective their service is going to be. On LearningToGive.org, Pat Nanzer says, "[Communities require] that people be knowledgeable about public issues and possess the capacity to work toward solution by acting together...working together to right injustices, change directions and pursue benefits for the common good." Solving public issues is a civic duty. One can also obtain their goals by working with a group who share the same thought-process. Doing something with passion and will without wanting something in turn is the way to be socially responsible.

Social responsibility is prominent for many reasons. It helps to create a better environment for everyone. David Meltzer, on entrepreneur.com, comments, "...how important the practice [of social responsibility] is to a person's emotional well-being... the person that is receiving[.] ...[and] anyone who witnesses...experiences the same... benefits..." The people serving, receiving, and witnessing feel the same happiness. On inc.com, Martin Zwilling shares, "[Social responsibility] improves your team motivation and productivity..." With this, a community will thrive. Finally, Jason A. Pedwell, on linkedin.com, posted, "By actively participating in local causes not only does a company build local rapport with the community which ultimately translates to higher levels of trust and brand recognition, the causes that they support also have a direct impact on the quality of life for residents." It's proven that social responsibility improves lives. Participation in local causes leave good influences for others to follow. Decisively, one should be an active member so that the other citizens can enjoy their communities.

Attitude and ethics is important in social responsibility. The performance of a person reflects off their mood. To be civically responsible, one must have good working ethics. Naomi Enevoldson, a social-entrepreneur, writes on her website, imasocialentrepeneur.com, "...[one] must behave ethically and with sensitivity toward social, cultural, economic and environmental issues." Basically, the best way to help the community is to do something one truly cares for to help their community. You must also behave tranquilly. Wendy Taylor-Loftus, on quora.com, said that "Social responsibility is, behaving in a manner which promotes peace, safety and well-being for all humankind." One should be safe while being helpful and that they need to be peaceful. Aggression never works in responsibility. Citizens must be ready to learn and be open to new things. Overall, a soft and peaceful personality is required to be of help to others.

Many people think that civic responsibility is just a 'burden' you hold for others. In his blog, Mallen Baker's Respectful Business Blog, Mallen Baker writes, "We do not live in a Disney world where virtue is always seen to be rewarded, and that's a fact." What he is saying is that one may not always get something by helping others. And since one might not receive anything financially or tangibly, they shouldn't do it. He also says that volunteering won't get anybody anywhere. On toughnickel.com, Drea DeFoe claims that it's not the companies' jobs to help others. "...businesses should focus on profits and let the government or nonprofit organizations deal with social and environmental issues." She says that businesses shouldn't even tie in with the society unless needed for its personal benefits. Drea later explains that employees can't work their best and be socially responsible at the same time. This is practically another way of saying that helping others is a waste of time which interferes with your schedule and your performance when it's completely unnecessary. Her far-reaching words mean that supporting a social cause is a waste of time, effort and money, all which are very valuable. So, is social responsibility a good thing or is it bad? As many people say that helping others is a responsibility that every human should acquire as a must-do job, there a lot of others who claim that the best thing to do is mind their own business.

Social responsibility varies from smaller to larger deeds. Some people help others cross the road while other volunteer in places like classrooms. In my previous school, a Color-Run and a Jog-A-Thon were held annually to fund school supplies and activities. The students took an active part in raising funds and participating. Some local companies like Ocean Mist and Dole supported the school by donating money and supplies also. Then, there is an accessible park named Tatum's Garden in Monterey Bay. This park was designed by several kids' ideas, including mine and my brother's, and volunteers working together to make it a reality. It was a great feeling to give back to the community. Another great example is Martin Luther King Jr. who helped bring social justice and equality. He helped his fellow citizens have better living and working conditions. Many more events like these occur in our country and society.

Civic duty is an option in which you are willing to assist your community so that it prospers. Naomi Enevoldson articulates that it "…helps [by having] a positive impact …" These people bring social justice to their community. And they have no other goal but to help the American society advance and strive. Being socially responsible means trying to improve conditions by intentions to assist the citizens. Americans should be socially responsible by improving their community, exhibiting good work ethics, knowing what the issues are, and doing what they enjoy.

Works Cited

Baker, Mallen. "Arguments against Corporate Social Responsibility - And Some Responses." Mallen Baker's Respectful Business Blog, 22 May 2008, mallenbaker.net/article/clear-reflection/arguments-against-corporate-social-responsibility-and-some-responses.

DeFoe, Drea. "Arguments for and Against Corporate Social Responsibility." ToughNickel, ToughNickel, 24 June 2015, toughnickel.com/business/Arguments-for-and-Against-Corporate-Social-Responsibility.

Dragonette, Laura. "Social Responsibility." Investopedia, 7 June 2017, www.investopedia.com/terms/s/socialresponsibility.asp.

Hayzlett, Jeffrey. "Why Should Your Business Care About Social Responsibility?" Entrepreneur, 10 October 2016, www.entrepreneur.com/article/269665.

Meltzer, David. "The Masters of Giving." Entrepreneur, 25 December 2017, www.entrepreneur.com/article/306581.

Nanzer, Pat. "Individual Rights and Community Responsibilities." Individual Rights and Community Responsibilities | Learning to Give, www.learningtogive.org/resources/individual-rights-and-community-responsibilities.

"Our Individual Social Responsibility Essay." Our Individual Social Responsibility Essay - 408 Palabras | Cram, www.cram.com/essay/our-individual-social-responsibility/FKCVYL2SC.

Pedwell, Jason A. "7 Reasons You Should Care About Social Responsibility." Linkedin.com, 20 September 2014 https://www.linkedin.com/pulse/20140920064507-22023966-7-reasons-you-should-care-about-social-responsibility.

"Social Responsibility and Ethics | Who Is Responsible And Why?" Who Is Responsible And Why? | Pachamama Alliance, www.pachamama.org/social-justice/social-responsibility-and-ethics.

The Citizen's Almanac: Fundamental Documents, Symbols, and Anthems of the United States. U.S. Dept. of Homeland Security, U.S. Citizenship and Immigration Services, 2014.

"What is social Responsibility" Quora - Quora https://www.quora.com/ What-is-social-responsibility www.facebook.com/naomiene. "What Is Social Responsibility?" Naomi Enevoldson - Social Entrepreneur, 27 April 2012, www.imasocialentrepreneur.com/social-responsibility/.

Zwilling, Martin. "8 Reasons Why Being Socially Responsible Is Good For Business." Inc.com, Inc., www.inc.com/martin-zwilling/8-reasons-why-being-socially-responsible-is-good-for-business.html.

Social Responsibility

Vaishvi Joshi
Fruitvale Junior High School

A seventh grader at Fruitvale Junior High, Vaishvi Joshi is a bright student. She has won many awards including Science Fair, and Oral Language, and was the Top Student in Accelerated Reader in her elementary school. She also won the Henry Greve Speech Contest, in which the topic was "Traits of a Successful Person." She enjoys reading and hanging out with her friends on the weekends.

૭

Dr. T. Haynes in his book, Social Responsibility and Organizational Ethics, defined social responsibility as a direct or an indirect obligation of an individual through which this whole society is benefited. I feel it is a responsibility of every individual to contribute in the positive development of our society. Through the random acts of kindness, we can help the welfare of our society. After reading articles of Dr. Robert James and Dr. Kalinda in Encyclopedia of Business and Finance, we, as students, can contribute toward a meaningful impact in three ways. First, by avoiding, or not engaging in harmful activities. Second, by creating a positive developmental environment, and third, performing activities, which advance the societies' progressive goals.

First we need to avoid or not engage in harmful activities. Picasso once said, "All children are artists. The problem is how to remain an artist once he grows up." This, I believe is the central problem in the life of children. Students and kids are facing challenges to be cool. For example the game, Truth or Dare, in which someone asks you a personal question that you have to answer truthfully or a dare that you have to do even if you don't want to. Another example is the salt and ice challenge, in which you have to pour salt onto some part of your body before placing an ice cube over the salted area. Then the kids post pictures of their burns on social media. They do it as a dare or challenge and want to do it to fit in the other cool kids. Another example is that kids fall for stuff they see on the Internet. They think if the kids online are doing it, it must be okay to do it too. The Internet contains helpful ideas as well as harmful or inappropriate things for kids and teens.

Students fall in trap of Internet. For example, students go on a certain website for school research, then they see an ad that is tempting, and their mind is diverted from the main focus. Students then keep jumping from one website to other and can get virus in their computers' which results in the theft of personal information. This can hurt their family and in turn the society. Another example of engaging in harmful activities arises from social media. The American Academy of Pediatrics has warned about the potential negative effects of social media in young kids and teens, including cyber-bullying and "Facebook depression." Other concerns are loss of privacy because with everything posted, there is a location shared. Even though you may have the opportunity to "private" your account, nothing is really private, everything is out there. This affects mental and emotional status of kids and their families. Students get lower grades due to the addiction to social media. Students nowadays are now scrolling through their friends' Instagram instead of studying for a test.

One would wonder how this is related to social responsibility, but if we think correctly, it is the social responsibility of a student to create a positive environment in the society. If the students or kids are exposed to such dangers, because of their acts, on the Internet, and social media, their families could suffer because kids are also part of a family. There could be a lot more arguments in the house, which can result in depression of kids. This may not only be dividing the family but, also causing anxiety and depression in the parents who are constantly worried about their kids. Thus if the parents and kids keep moving farther and farther away, how can we expect our society to flourish and grow? Indirectly, it is the social responsibility of a student to be aware of the harmful things which can hurt the development of our society.

Secondly kids and teens need to create a positive environment for themselves as well as the surrounding people. They need to be aware about the child maltreatment happening everywhere including physical, emotional and sexual abuse as well as neglect. They have to focus on their studies at school and make sure that there is no-bullying. Bullying causes depression, anxiety, increased feelings of sadness and loneliness, changes in sleep and eating patterns, and loss of interest in activities they used to enjoy, and sometimes even suicide. Kids don't feel like living because of the hate they are given. They feel pressured or stressed which is harming our society and community. That's why we have to raise awareness and create nurturing relationships with each other in our own community.

One way to do that is to become more connected with the society, or in other words, volunteer. We, kids, can help in public libraries and churches as well as keep the local parks and schools clean. Children who are smart in studies can also form after-school math tutoring clubs. We also have to support each other as a community. Altogether we can offer our neighbors some support. We can get to know them better and they'll probably return the favor too. It can be something simple like carrying the groceries from the car or getting the mail for them. Another way to become connected with the society is to raise money. We can give to the hospitals for all the sick or homeless. We can also donate old items, like clothes or toys to local charities. We can do almost anything. As John Dickinson has said, "United we stand, divided we fall."

When students and kids understand their social responsibility and the impact it can have, then the kids will get a broader perspective of what the problem is. When we know the problem, then only can it be treated so when the kids avoid harmful activities, that contributes to a positive environment in their home which would eventually create a positive impact on the whole society. Also, when the kids support each other by volunteering, coaching, teaching and standing next to each other shoulder to shoulder, this is creating a strong network in the society which will affect everyone. This would ultimately result in creating better teachers, better scientists, better engineers, and overall, better human beings.

Kids and students have an indirect social responsibility in creating a better future for our societies-to-be. Social responsibility not only means supporting our society in a positive beneficial way today, but also uplifting every human being so that everyone in the society can have a better tomorrow.

Works Cited

Brown, Jessica. "Future - Is Social Media Bad for You? The Evidence and the Unknowns." BBC, BBC, 5 Jan. 2018, www.bbc.com/future/story/20180104-is-social-media-bad-for-you-the-evidence-and-the-unknowns.

Friedman, Jenny. "Volunteer With Your Kids." Parents, Parents, 6 Dec. 2017, www.parents.com/parenting/better-parenting/style/volunteer-with-your-kids/.

Haynes, T. (n.d.). Social Responsibility and Organizational Ethics. Retrieved May 8, 2010, http://www.answers.com/topic/social-responsibility-and-organizational-ethics.

Ramsland, Katherine. "Dangerous Things Kids Do." Psychology Today, Sussex Publishers, 18 June 2017, www.psychologytoday.com/blog/shadow-boxing/201706/dangerous-things-kids-do.

Walton, Alice G. "6 Ways Social Media Affects Our Mental Health." Forbes, Forbes Magazine, 3 Oct. 2017, www.forbes.com/sites/alicegwalton/2017/06/30/a-run-down-of-social-medias-effects-on-our-mental-health/#211cc7d42e5a.

Social Responsibility

Cheyanne Pena
Lakeside School

Cheyanne Pena is an 8th grader at Lakeside Middle School. She is interested in Japanese culture and someday would like to visit Japan.

❦

"In a world of lies and liars, an honest work of art is always an act of social responsibility," says Robert McKee. Social responsibility in American society is built on a set of principles, or moral code, called ethics. Society is a large social group with self same geography and social territory. To be a socially responsible member of American society, one has a duty to contribute to the betterment of our world. One way to interface in society is to take only what is needed. An additional way is to help keep clean parks, streets, and neighborhoods. Ultimately, one's actions and decisions must benefit society.

To take only what one needs is an example of social responsibility. Akiroq Brost stated, "Buy what you need, use what you buy. Don't buy just for the sake of acquiring." Through conservation, individuals can reduce waste and manage natural resources wisely. Reducing water and electrical usage is a praiseworthy way to do just that. By donating untouched food, that would have otherwise gone to waste, one is doing a socially responsible act. In our society, there are many people who have to worry about where their next meal will come from but by donating food, one can help take that burden off them, resulting in a kinder more caring world.

Keeping parks, streets, and neighborhoods clean is part of one's duty as a member of society. Cleaning up after one's self is one way to do such.

Christine Pelosi stated, "Being green and clean is not just an aspiration but an action." Pollution is a rising threat to not only society, but to our world. If individuals were to recycle plastic, paper, and cardboard it could be later used for other commodities.

To be a socially responsible member of American society, one's actions and decisions must contribute to society, not solely to said individual. Maureen Ryan, a sexual health and wellness coach in Amherst, N.Y. stated, "People have a right to be selfish, to an extent, when making lifestyle changes in search of happiness, but in situations where other people are wholly dependent on you… it's not always appropriate to make yourself the priority." Others in society will be affected based on what you do or say, so with that in mind one must consider the consequences of one's actions and decisions before one does, to prevent harming anyone in the process. A safer and more educated world will be achieved by doing so. If the action or decision causes harm to society or the environment then it would be considered to be socially irresponsible.

When one acts in a manner that harms society rather than contributes to it, it's considered socially irresponsible. Laws are the binding principles of society. Breaking the law is an example of social irresponsibility. When one does not follow the laws, they may be punished for their crime with a fine or even jail time. Helping society is always the correct thing to do.

When one considers it, a socially responsible person is one who helps the community. Taking only what one needs conserves resources and helps more people alleviate difficulties. Cleaning local areas such as parks, streets, and neighborhoods reduces possibilities to pollution, ultimately helping Earth. Having one's actions and decisions benefit society contributes to the amelioration of said communities. So, based on the information, do you consider yourself to be a socially responsible member of American society?

What Does It Mean to Be a Socially Responsible Member of American Society?

Garrett Redstone
Fruitvale Junior High School

Garrett Redstone is 12 years old and is in the seventh grade at Fruitvale Jr. High. Garrett has had many accomplishments in language leading up to the Writers of Kern essay contest. Garrett has participated in oral language in fifth and sixth grade, placing second in the county for humorous duo with his partner, Alex Lopez. Garrett has also participated in this year's Henry Grieves Speech, making it to regionals with the topic, "What are the Traits of a Successful Person?" Garrett enjoys hobbies such as painting, drawing, reading, playing video games, and playing chess. He even participates in local chess tournaments and has placed in the top ten numerous times and even first place! Garrett is a great kid that hopes to do big things, and he's especially excited about this huge accomplishment printed on his college application.

To be a socially responsible member of American society is to be involved in your individual community and help it to blossom and grow. Living in a community is a promise to improve it by making a difference with the actions you make and the power your presence has for others living in your community. To be a socially responsible member of American society is to work hard for your nation and not expect anything in return. John F. Kennedy, a former American president, said in his inaugural address — "And so, my fellow Americans, ask not what your country can do for you -- ask what you can do for your country." This is a perfect guideline for those that strive to give back to their communities, as well as for those that are a bit apprehensive about it for it could give them the inspiration needed to get them started.

The decisions the President of the United States makes daily are for the well-being of every citizen in the country and directly influence every one of their lives. Community leaders also undertake similar duties but on a much smaller scale. It doesn't even have to be a community leader, it could be an average resident that happens to work a couple hours a week at the homeless shelter or picking up trash at a local park. People like this inspire others to do the same and lead the entire community to be a higher socially functioning society.

There are many ways to affect people's lives like fundraising for a family that has a loved one in the hospital or making a meal for those in need. Even little things like this can brighten someone's day and motivate them to do the same for someone else. Leaders keep repeating this and all of a sudden they've empowered the whole community to be a unified group of socially responsible individuals. Being a socially responsible member of American society means to take into consideration the needs of others and put them before your own. Acts of selflessness like these are what helps a community to come together for the common good.

If you have a passion, any passion, chances are there is going to be someone in need with that same passion. Being responsible means to take that passion and spread it like wildfire, motivate those around you, until change slowly comes around. Cesar Chavez accomplished this and gave farmworkers their well-deserved rights, against all odds too. He accomplished what was, back then, unthinkable simply by fighting for what he knew was right. He is a prime example of someone who was a socially responsible member of American society.

Socially responsible members of American society know their role in their communities and they fill it out. People like this don't always get the see the change that they've caused, but that might inspire even more to follow in their footsteps and live their legacy. A legacy is often measured in how much change you've brought to your community or larger society. As said by the songwriter Lin Manuel-Miranda, a legacy is "planting seeds in a garden you never get to see." If someone starts planting, but doesn't finish, chances are there's a socially responsible member of American society that will tend to it till it bears its fruits. A socially responsible member of American society will fill out another's legacy or start their own for the sake of change.

Works Cited

"How to Get Involved." Corporation for National and Community Service, www.nationalservice.gov/serve-your-community/how-get-involved.

Making a Difference:How to Become and Remain Active in Your Community. http://www.state.sc.us/dmh/client_affairs/volunteer_guide.pdf.

2019

High School

The Library: A Symbolic Survivor

Kaylee Choe
Stockdale High School

Kaylee Choe is currently a senior at Stockdale High School. She is 17 years old, plays and coaches soccer, and is planning to attend Cal Poly- San Luis Obispo in the fall to study Environmental Protection. Kaylee enjoys writing, theatre, soccer, and volunteering at her school to give back to the community. She dedicates her academic successes to her closest friends and family, especially her two younger brothers and younger sister, who she hopes to inspire to always try their best in their future endeavors.

I still remember my feelings of wonder when entering the public library with my dad when I was eight years old. Seeing the tall shelves continue on for what seemed like forever always excited me. My dad was young, single, and could not afford to buy me all the books I wanted to read, so we began making trips to the public library. During these visits, he'd allow me to lose myself in my reading and to check out however many books I wanted. In today's society, public libraries face the stereotype of being quiet and boring. However, they are much more than uneventful buildings where books are held. They are sanctuaries for pre-Internet Era thinking and provide relief from the constantly fast-paced nature of the Internet Era. Attention-grabbing ads and posts on social media that shove content into the viewer's face are unable to penetrate the library's walls. In this way, this lone survivor of pre-Internet Era practices serves as a symbol to today's society of the clash between the technology-driven future and the reminiscent past.

Despite their survival, libraries have simultaneously faced the struggles of decreases in attendance and having to compete with society's growing obsession with social media. Between 2012 and 2015, visits to public libraries dropped a whole 9%, from 53% to 44% (Horrigan). This significant drop in attendance for a period of three years expresses the decreasing popularity in libraries among the nation. A decrease in attendance this sudden could also present new financial challenges to public libraries, with less popularity comes the risk of less funding. Competing with the ever-growing threat of social media is another struggle public libraries must face. Social media use in recent years has dramatically spiked in number and intensity. The use of Instagram among U.S. adults has increased by 7% in two years and the percentage of users who would find it difficult to give up their social media has risen from 28% to 40% in four years (Smith and Anderson). People in today's society dedicate a growing amount of time to social media, creating less time and desire for practices such as reading by throwing entertaining and convenient content in users' faces. Technological advances have created changes in the minds and priorities of average people, leading to an inclination towards convenient entertainment such as social media and a disinclination towards libraries and reading.

While libraries continue to deal with challenges in today's society, the access and sense of community they provide are ultimately what keeps them afloat. Not everyone has home access to the Internet, which is now necessary for many people and activities. In fact, according to Pew Research Center, only about 65% of U.S. adults use high-speed Internet in their home (Pewinternet. org). Luckily for the remaining 35% of American adults, a report managed by the American Library Association states 98% of all libraries offer free public WiFi (Ala.org). This allows those without easy Internet access in their homes to not fall behind in a society where the internet plays an increasingly important role. Internet access is especially critical to young adults without home internet due to the college-application process being almost exclusively online. Along with providing for those with limited opportunities, public libraries also provide a sense of community. Currently, Kern County's own Beale Library is hosting multiple events for the community- a ukulele club, craft activities for both children and adults, and Halloween-themed events (kclevents.org). These events allow the residents of Kern County to meet new people with similar interests, developing not only personal relationships but the sense of unity among the community as well. Advances in technology may increase the desire for convenience in today's society, but technology's lack of accessibility and its inability to quench the human desire for a sense of community are the reasons libraries continue to thrive in the technological era.

The struggles and successes libraries face today reveal more than why they are one of the last remaining pre-technological era industries left; they also reveal the true role of the public library in the Internet Era. The public library serves as a symbol- a manifestation of the continuous war between modern-age technology, its impacts on society, and more traditional behaviors and values, often lost or changed because of the rate at which society is changing. These include the struggles between the technology-induced craving for convenience among consumers and the human desire for community and social interaction as well as the addictively entertaining content of social media and the human mind's thirst for intellectual stimulation. These conflicting priorities and desires can be physically expressed through the survival of the library. The public library symbolizes society's paradoxical goal of progress and desire for tradition.

Works Cited

Anderson, Monica, and Smith, Aaron, "Social Media Use in 2018," Social Media Use in 2018, Pew Internet & American Life Project, March 1, 2018, http://www.pewinternet.org/2018/03/01/social-media-use-in-2018/, accessed on October 6, 2018. Pg 7

"Events for October 2018 › Beale." Kern County Library, https://kclevents. org/events/category/beale/.

Horrigan, John B., "2. Library Usage and Engagement," Libraries 2016, Pew Internet & American Life Project, September 9, 2016, http://www. pewinternet.org/2016/09/09/library-usage-and-engagement/, accessed on October 6, 2018. Pg 11.

"Internet Access and Digital Holdings in Libraries," American Library Association, September 26, 2006, http://www.ala.org/tools/libfactsheets/ alalibraryfactsheet26 (Accessed October 6, 2018).

"Internet/Broadband Fact Sheet," Pew Research Center, February 5, 2018. http://www.pewinternet.org/fact-sheet/internet-broadband/ (Accessed October 6, 2018).

Libraries in the Digital Age

Grace Spoelstra
Bakersfield Christian High School

Public libraries are important to keep while our society is changing so fast for they offer opportunities that today's electronic advances can't provide. Although what they extend to the public can be found easily on any computer, tablet, or phone, it's the feeling that it provides that keeps the masses from turning away from a tradition and allows for escape from the technological era.

Public libraries provide a community that can not be provided by any device. The Orland Park Public Library provides an example of the schedule of a public library and how it shows how easily accessible it is. While one may just think that a person can only access books and desks for tutoring, the information filled building in fact provides activities for all ages. For families looking for some quality time together, including a sort of activeness, there are many options. Community service, active workouts, and babysitting are just a few examples that are available at various hours.

With this constant upgrading world, traditional atmospheres are important to keep as options. The former president of the American Library Association, Nancy Kranich, describes the original purpose of libraries as being an informal education center. But with the right to attend school, libraries are no longer needed as an educational center although they are used as extra support for students. Jenny Shank, states that libraries today provide a center for Hispanics, people without high school diplomas, those unemployed, rural Americans, and people with incomes less than 30,000 since they are less likely to participate in electronic options like E-books. They hold a special educational value that citizens cannot gain from the internet.

Although citizens may think it is a waste of space as we move into a world where everything can be accessed online, it is important to provide a place like a library for many reasons. Those who are unfortunate to be able to have the luxury of having electronic devices to read, use the library for solitude when having the need to study. Libraries provide a place for individuals to meet and participate in activities. Many even allow for daycare making it easier for families. With so many options, libraries are unrated while the advances of technology over pass them. Having a traditional study atmosphere helps students and young adults escape from the busy and very distracting luxuries of home or work.

What Is the Role of the Public Library in the Internet Era?

Anna Underwood
Bakersfield Christian High School

This is Anna's second time to compete in the Young Writers of Kern Essay competition, and her second winning essay. Her first experience and win in 2017 was a highlight of her 7th grade year, and Anna is thrilled to be a part of this inspiring competition a second time. She would like to thank her mentor, English teacher Mrs. Leslie Stump, who encouraged her to develop her essay writing skills. Besides writing, Anna competes in Forensics with BCHS. She would like to be an English teacher or an attorney.

The public library has long been a haven for book enthusiasts of all kinds. It originally was created for the purpose of collecting books for access by the general public, to be used for reading or study purposes. Historically, public libraries were intended to keep the business, legal, religious and historical records of civilization. The types of information and literature one could find at a public library were unparalleled anywhere else, besides the few--but vast and largely inaccessible--private libraries owned by the wealthy. As time went on, the library evolved to include specialized materials, such as books designed specifically for the blind, as well as for those visually or hearing impaired. Whole sections were created for audio and videos, often with a nominal fee to cover replacement costs on these new forms of media that could be used up more quickly than a printed book. Then came computers and the Internet Era, and the library systems began to adjust their offerings again.

The computer age was embraced by the public library systems in America.

Word processors, then computers, and even printers were made available to the public. Later, when the Internet became an important resource, the libraries designated computers with internet access, where within a set time limit, one could browse the internet for free to their heart's content.

The internet brought with it a new way to obtain information that had previously only been available at public libraries or specialized research facilities. Although the internet was not free, the public increasingly found ways to access it cheaply. Places like Starbuck's began to offer free internet to its guests to encourage them to stay longer and purchase more, which meant that free libraries began to share the load of free internet access. The question began to arise that with all of the avenues to access news, resources, and information via the internet, has the public library become redundant?

The public library system as an institution retains its importance to our society in spite of the Internet Era, because it maintains itself as a reliably credible source for all kinds of research and media, and has been able to remain free or affordable to its targeted constituency.

There are a number of reasons that support this statement. For instance, when it comes to research, the accuracy of what can be found on the internet is less reliable than the well-curated information provided at the public library. Encyclopedia-style websites such as Wikipedia.com are not only used by the public to obtain information on a topic quickly, but are also added to and published by the general public, and this information is not properly verified. Furthermore, in spite of the fact that a large percentage of society has access to the internet, there is still a cost that is prohibitive to the less-advantaged percentage. It is costly to digitize books. Audiobooks usually cost more than the actual book purchase. Even if you can afford easy access, medical journals, legal documents, and other valuable materials are still expensive in online media, and often still only exist in book form. The public libraries are run and paid for with our tax dollars, allowing for free admission to all residents.

Some might claim that the public library system is not longer providing a value to the public. They may even claim that our tax dollars are being wasted on nothing more than a sentimental monument to a need that is long past.

However, these claims completely fail to recognize that these "wasted" tax dollars are feeding the public's ongoing need for materials they could not find free anywhere else. Furthermore, the "sentimental monument" is also a trusted monument, and for good reason. The public library is a free and credible way to gather information. Roly Keeting, director of the British Library, said in

2015 that "[t]hey stand for private study in a social space; they are safe, they're places of sanctuary and play a vital role in some of the poorest communities. And they are trusted."

The public library is vitally important to the disadvantaged community who don't have any access to the internet. Accessing the internet can be a costly investment, unlike the public library, which is provided by the state and paid for by the taxes of the community. Because as Rani Molla confirms from Red-code, "In the U.S., that disparity isn't as wide. About 23 percent of people in urban areas don't have access to or can't afford broadband versus 28 percent in rural areas." This percentage of Americans who "don't have access to or can't afford" the internet are given a quality, credible, safe haven labeled as the public library. The original intent of public libraries was to provide the poor with access to the same academic knowledge as the wealthy. Then and now, people with no money could just go and sit in a public library and read to their hearts' content.

Judging the reliability of the information published on the web is critical for many types of research, and there are no laws or official institutions tasked with verifying the reliability of what is found on the internet. The internet functions as really more of a huge "open air market" than a trusted keeper of valuable resources. There are no Internet regulations to keep time sensitive or important-but-evolving data and information updated on a regular basis. People expect a published book on an important topic to be properly researched and edited by those who understand the subject. As Abigail Geiger from the Pew Research Center indicates, "a majority of Americans say public libraries are helpful as people try to meet their information needs." In Abigail's interviews, she questioned multiple age groups, and the majority of her subjects confirmed that the general public believes the public library system is more of a credible source than the Internet. The public library carefully picks and catalogues what is put on their shelves. Readers and researchers can find multiple credible sources in one place for a variety of research projects.

It must be acknowledged that the internet has come to be an essential way of living in the technological era, such that it may be our main or only source of some types of information. However, this does not negate the enduring value of the public library institution. It cannot be denied that the public library system still has a necessary role in the Internet era. The public library remains a great equalizer in our society. It is reliable, credible, organized, and geared toward the needs of society. Mr. Keating stated, "With all our fascination of and love for the internet in the age of data, these values and the values and idea of the library predated the internet and if we get it right may yet outlast it." For these reasons, we should all support continued funding for the continuation of our public libraries and the stabilizing and trustworthy service they provide to our communities.

Work Cited

Estabrook, Leigh S. "Library." Encyclopedia Britannica, inc. October 30, 2018, https://www.britannica.com/topic/library.

Furness, Hannah. "Libraries could outlast the internet, head of British Library says." Telegraph. May 25, 2015, https://www.telegraph.co.uk/culture/hay-festival/11627276/Libraries-could-outlast-the-internet-head-of-British-Library-says.html.

Sturgis Library. "Mirror mirror on the wall, who's the OLDEST of them all…?" Sturgis Library; Barnstable, Massachusetts. October 27, 2018, http://www.sturgislibrary.org/history/oldest-library/.

Herring Mark Y. "Despite public demand, the notion persists with some that the internet makes libraries unnecessary." American Libraries. October 25, 2018, https://americanlibrariesmagazine.org/2010/01/20/10-reasons-why-the-internet-is-no-substitute-for-a-library/.

Geiger, Abigail. "Most Americans – especially Millennials – say libraries can help them find reliable, trustworthy information." Pew Research center. October 28, 2018, http://www.pewresearch.org/fact-tank/2017/08/30/most-americans-especially-millennials-say-libraries-can-help-them-find-reliable-trustworthy-information/.

Molla, Rani. "Population density in cities means the story isn't rosy despite higher connectivity rates." Recode. October 23, 2018, https://www.recode.net/2017/6/20/15839626/disparity-between-urban-rural-internet-access-major-economies.

Middle School

The Role of the Public Library in the Internet Era

Simone Basilio
Fruitvale Junior High School

Simone Basilio is an eighth grader at Fruitvale Junior High School and will be attending Frontier High School. Born in Bakersfield, Simone and her family lived in Manchester, England for several years before returning to her native city two years ago. A loyal fan of Manchester United Football Club, Simone also has many hobbies, among them being reading and drawing, exploring public libraries and museums, and spending time with her pet corgi, Hiro. Simone is passionate about social activism and dreams of becoming a professor in Sociology.

৯

Public libraries around the world share the common goal of granting their patrons with access to resources and materials and providing them with the necessary tools to achieve an equal chance of success. University and other special libraries may help their patrons achieve similar goals, but they do not necessarily provide equal access for everyone. For these reasons, the public library holds an important and significant place in modern society. In this digital age, public libraries can provide a much more fulfilling experience than the Internet by being social hubs in a community and a retreat for the individual.

However, there are those who claim that libraries are becoming unnecessary or even obsolete in the modern, digital age. Just recently, for example, an Economics professor published an op-ed in Forbes magazine, arguing for the replacement of public libraries with Amazon stores. Professor Mourdoukoutas contended that public libraries are becoming unreasonable and "don't have the same value they used to" (Ha, 2018). For him, the services libraries used to provide have been replaced: "community and wifi are now provided by Starbucks; video rentals by Netflix and Amazon Prime; and books by Amazon" (Ha, 2018). Furthermore, communities which fund the public libraries through local taxes are also better served by Amazon bookstores because they do not take taxpayers' money. While Mourdoukoutas does make a point that some may agree with, there are still many reasons that public libraries remain key places in a community.

The publics' response was swift and severe. Many people and public librarians all over the world immediately took to Twitter to express their displeasure. "Libraries are not simply book repositories," one tweeted, "they are a place where communities can come together, exchange ideas and tackle local issues. A Starbucks or an Amazon store do none of these things." Another clarified, "My Los Angeles Public Library card allows me access to all you mentioned and more. Today we offered a genealogy workshop, indigenous writers conference, puppet show, tai chi class and travel craft in one location. My cost in taxes? 37 CENTS." The Forbes article was soon deleted (Ha, 2018). It is clear that public libraries still matter to many, as majority of the passionate responses to the Forbes article suggest.

Indeed, a public library serves the community. Librarians and library services do more than just check out books. They also help their patrons navigate social services, aging, mental health, welfare and public assistance, housing resources, health care, and education and employment resources (Cabello and Butler, 2017). Many libraries, particularly in poor communities, have anti-hunger and feeding programs for children. These libraries tap into the community by recruiting volunteers, conducting fundraising activities, and coordinating with local businesses and non-profit organizations. In 2016, public libraries in California provided over 203,000 meals for many underprivileged children (Saint Louis, 2017). By providing these meals, children are physically nourished while at the same time become more engaged with other programs the library has to offer.

It is amazing that local libraries here in Kern County have diverse programs and workshops that cater to different groups of people with various needs and interests. These include teen acting, social media, computer basics, and many others. Specifically, the Beale Memorial Library organizes programs not only for children and teens, but also veterans and immigrants. They have literacy programs for those who are deficient in English and suicide prevention programs discussing PTSD for veterans (Broderick, 2018). Although some may argue that these skills or ideas may be learned online, an important part is the social aspect of attending a workshop in real life, where one can meet new people and exchange ideas on both a public and personal level.

According to a Pew survey from 2013, 95% of Americans ages 16 and older agree that the materials and resources available at public libraries play an important role in giving everyone a chance to succeed (Purcell et al., 2013). The public library provides everyone in its community, not just those with financial resources, an equal opportunity to information and access to community resources. Thus, libraries are not just simply a place for recreational reading, but rather a place for people to meet and come together and help each other out as a community.

Public libraries can also become a sanctuary place for the individual. In my personal experience, libraries have always provided me with a safe space where I could always feel comfortable. This experience in a public library is not just limited to the libraries in my city, but in other places in the world. For the few years I lived in Manchester, England, going to the library was also a gratifying experience. I shared the same feeling that I feel in Bakersfield's public libraries: feelings of welcoming, belonging and warmth. When I see people of different walks of life together in a library, it gives me a feeling of happiness and joy. No matter who you are, you are always welcome in a public library. Even though I have access to the Internet with all the answers and information I could ever want, I still make the choice to go to the library.

In conclusion, even in the age of the Internet, it is for some of these aforementioned reasons that people still find public libraries an important part of the community and everyday life. Public libraries play an important role in educating and supporting their communities. This can be from lending out books, to assisting those who need help finding jobs, and even those dealing with traumatic experiences. They do not discriminate. Public libraries are crucial to maintaining a healthy and safe community for all.

Works Cited

Broderick, Kelly. "Beale Memorial Library Holding Veteran Suicide Prevention Discussion." 23ABC News, 4 Sept. 2018, www.turnto23.com/news/local-news/beale-memorial-library-holding-veteran-suicide-prevention-discussion.

Ha, Thu-Huong. "Forbes Deleted a Deeply Misinformed Op-Ed Arguing Amazon Should Replace Libraries." Quartz, Quartz, 23 July 2018, qz.com/1334123/forbes-deleted-an-op-ed-arguing-that-amazon-should-replace-libraries/.

Louis, Catherine Saint. "Free Lunch at the Library." The New York Times, The New York Times, 30 July 2017, www.nytimes.com/2017/07/30/well/family/free-lunch-at-the-library.html.

Lyons, Kate. "'Twaddle': Librarians Respond to Suggestion Amazon Should Replace Libraries." The Guardian, Guardian News and Media, 23 July 2018, www.theguardian.com/books/2018/jul/23/twaddle-librarians-respond-to-suggestion-amazon-should-replace-libraries.

Purcell, Kristen, et al. "Part 1: The Role of Libraries in People's Lives and Communities." Pew Research Center: Internet, Science & Tech, Pew Research Center: Internet, Science & Tech, 22 Jan. 2013, www.pewinternet.org/2013/01/22/part-1-the-role-of-libraries-in-peoples-lives-and-communities/.

What is the Role of the Public Library in the Internet Era?

Garrett Redstone
Fruitvale Junior High School

Garrett Redstone is a very short 13-year-old in the eighth grade attending Fruitvale Jr. High. He has previously won the Young Writers of Kern essay competition in the seventh grade. He enjoys writing brief biographical sketches not exceeding 100 words and art, in particular, drawing. He is very involved in the mock trial and robotics programs at Fruitvale Jr. High, as well as several extracurricular activities. Garrett also has a knack for signing publishing agreements and attaching them to an e-mail with essays and biographical sketches.

The library dates back more than two-thousand years. An ancient concept of keeping knowledge stored in one place for everyone to access and grow from has survived for centuries, passed on through the generations. And yet, this genius place of learning has essentially been pushed to the back-burner with the invention of the internet. Where a library only has so much room to store physical copies of books, a cell phone holds all of them within one's hand. But, despite this, the public library still plays an important role in society.

Some may argue the internet gives all the information that one could need and that libraries are therefore useless. But, not all information on the internet is true. The library has been forced to change and evolve with the times and most notably with the internet being at the forefront of modern society. According to Wendy Philpott, Christine McWebb, a professor and director of academic programs at The University of Waterloo in Stratford says "...the library's role is changing and expanding from acquisition and storing of information to curation and quality control," (Philpott). This means libraries now specialize in deciding the quality and truthfulness of information in addition to the storing of it.

The Reading Agency is a group "Tackling life's big challenges through the proven power of reading." The blog found on their website says, "We all need libraries. They are the safe and trusted spaces in every community where we have free access not just to books, information, experiences and ideas but to the expert professional advice and support which we all need to help us find the resources we want and to use them effectively," (The Reading Agency).

Libraries give children access to thousands of books, allowing them not only to improve their literacy but also imagination. Wendy Philpott reports that McWebb believes libraries now serve as places where "knowledge is transformed into creativity," (Philpott).

When one starts to read, they are swept into the world in the pages. They witness scenarios that make their heart race and their breathing heavy. They relate with and start to love the book's characters and hate their antagonists. Readers are subjected to irony, suspense, surprise, wonder, magic, war, peace, happiness, despair, grief, amusement, adventure, mystery, hatred (especially towards Umbridge), fear, anger, death, life, friendship, heroes, villains, traitors, rivalry, secrets—and the list goes on— all due to bits of ink spelling out words on a piece of paper. Reading is essential to the blossoming of imagination, one of the most important qualities to possess in society. After all, imagination is essential to innovation and innovation is the key to progress of humans as a species.

However, reading can also improve an adults' literacy, making job opportunities for them by making them seem more mature and qualified by the word choices they use during an interview or even a resume. Some libraries even offer free literacy and computer classes. Computer skills also open job opportunities for adults both young and old.

Others may claim that libraries are now made obsolete by the invention of audio and digital books, but libraries give access to hundreds of thousands of books with an extremely inexpensive card, while when using audio or e-books one must pay full price for every book they want to read. In addition, e-books offer a storage file for books, but libraries offer places and buildings with safe, quiet environments to read or study. According to research by David Ferrer, many still prefer the feeling and functionality of a physical book and some have developed a nostalgia for them. Libraries then serve as sources for that nostalgia and remain important those who prefer physical books (Ferrer).

Libraries are safe places for people to come and learn within their communities. They both help create jobs for librarians, but also prepare adults, both young and old, with basic skills needed to obtain a job as well. Libraries also give people an inexpensive option to improve their literacy and creativity and provide countless individuals with entertainment and nostalgia through books. On top of this, librarians help us to obtain vital and reliable information for any project or research. Though the library does not play the same role as it once did, it has a substantial and essential role nonetheless.

Works Cited

Best_Schools. "50 Reasons Real Books Are Vastly Superior to Ebooks." TheBestSchools.org, Thebestschools.org, 19 June 2017, thebestschools. org/magazine/real-books-superior-ebooks/.

"Do Libraries Still Matter in the Age of Google?" Waterloo Stories, 29 Sept. 2014, uwaterloo.ca/stories/do-libraries-still-matter-age-google.

"The Reading Agency." Why We All Need Libraries | Reading Agency, readingagency.org.uk/news/blog/why-we-all-need-libraries.html.

The Roles of the Public Library in the Internet Era

Darcy Tang

Lakeside School

Darcy Tang grew up in Bakersfield, California. She attended Donald E. Suburu Elementary School and Lakeside Middle School. Her dream college is UCSF. When Darcy grows up, she wishes to become a cardiothoracic surgeon. When she was two-years-old, she had a heart leakage and she needed to stay in the hospital, since she needed surgery. The surgery was a success, and she continues to be grateful to the surgeons that performed the surgery on her. Her experience when she was two-years-old led to her dream of becoming a cardiothoracic surgeon.

∾

Have you ever been to a public library? Well, I have, and it was a great experience. The public library has important roles in the Internet Era and they are to give people the privilege to check out books, to access technology, and to help the community. Public libraries have existed even before we were born. They have changed massively over the years.

One role of the public library in the Internet Era is to give people the privilege to check out books. According to the article, "Why Public Libraries Matter: And How They Can Do More" by David Vinjamuri, it states," When you come into our library, we don't want you to be able to leave without borrowing. Our greatest compliment is when someone comes in for a neighborhood block watch meeting and leaves with an armload of books that they can't pass up. That's all merchandising." The public libraries allow people under the poverty line to check out books to increase their knowledge. People who can't afford to pay for expenses for education can go to the public library and learn more with the books that the library provides to the community.

Another role of the public library in the Internet Era is to allow people to access technology. Some people under the poverty line cannot afford to buy technology. In the article, "The Library Card" by Deborah Fallows, it states, "Many people rely on libraries for their computer and Internet use." Additionally, the article, "Why Public Libraries Matter: And How They Can Do More" by David Vinjamuri supports this idea. It says, "They used this access, among other purposes to find work, apply to college, secure government benefits, or to learn more about medical treatment." People can also use computers at the public libraries for homework.

Finally, the public library must help the community in the Internet Era. In the article, "The Library Card" by Deborah Fallows, it states, "In libraries, I have practiced yoga and tai chi, sipped lattes in coffee shops, and watched Millennials with laptops arrange their virtual startup offices at long reading-room tables." Libraries have classes and meetings. People can take classes to help their literacy. The community can meet up and discuss things with each other and get advice from the librarians.

It is clear that the role of the public library is very important in the Internet Era. The amount of public libraries need to increase, so people everywhere can check out books easily. People can access technology to apply for jobs and colleges. People in the community can have meetings at the public library. The role of the public library has become more advanced in the Internet Era. The community depends on the future of public libraries.

The Importance of Libraries in the Internet Era

Aidan Worthington
Fruitvale Junior High School

Aidan Aaron Worthington is a 7th grade student who attends Fruitvale Junior High. He prides himself on being a straight A student and is a member of the California Junior Scholarship Federation. He is an avid and voracious reader, enjoys writing, likes to participate in academic, extracurricular activities, and plays soccer. Aidan wants to become a fictional author when he grows up. Aidan was born on October 8, 2006 in San Luis Obispo, California and moved to Bakersfield when he was 3 years old. Aidan lives with his father, mother, and younger brother.

క

Libraries are still important, even today in the Internet Era. Public libraries are used for many things. Some of these things include education, information, individual improvement, and recreation. This essay will show the continuous importance of libraries.

The Internet is helpful, however, the public library is better. A counterclaim against this statement could be that the internet has more information. According to Joyce B. Radcliffe, a Serials Librarian, "ALA reports that only 8% of all journals and even fewer books are on the Internet. The most reliable scholarly information is available in books and journals" (Radcliffe). This means that public libraries have a more diverse selection of books than the Internet. People might also argue that more people have access to the Internet than the library. This also is not true. According to Statista, about 76.2% of the U.S. population accessed the Internet as of 2016. As of 2017, according to Mashable, the population of the United States was about 325.7 million people. That means about 248.2 million people accessed the Internet. This means that not all people can access the Internet because of many reasons, including people may not be able to afford it. A library card is free, as long as an individual doesn't lose it, and to get one, individuals only need an I.D. such as a fishing license, hunting license, driver's license, listing in the phone directory, or a property tax statement, according to the article, "How do I get a library card? How much do they cost?" This means almost everyone can get a library card. The Internet has a lot of information, but the library has more information and is easier to access.

Libraries are important even though the population now has access to the Internet. Libraries are better and more reliable than the Internet. They have an advantage for information due to their long history. According to the article "Public Libraries," the first public library, founded by Benjamin Franklin and some of his friends, was founded in 1731. The World Wide Web, when the whole world could use the Internet, was created in 1989, according to Pew Research Center, libraries are 258 years older. This gives libraries a huge advantage when it comes to how much longer it has been around. Libraries are also more reliable due to the fact that the Internet is unorganized while the library is organized. Radcliffe says that "There is not a system that catalogs and organizes all resources on the Internet. A search on the Internet is similar to searching an unclassified catalog. When people use any of the search engines, they're searching only part of the Internet. Searches are not always relevant to your topic and can cause a lot of wasted time, frustration and confusion." Access to knowledge that is credible is always better when it comes from sources in the library while the Internet can have websites with incorrect information.

The role of a library is important as it can provide help; Libraries provide help in many ways. One way is a librarian can help people find what they're looking for. Knowledgeable and friendly librarians are available to assist with locating information in person, chat, e-mail or telephone. If someone requests assistance at the beginning of research, they spare valuable time spent on the Internet. Radcliffe also says that online databases are also open 24/7. Libraries can also help because they contain a wide variety of books. If the library doesn't have the book someone is looking for they can request a book from another library. Getting books online isn't always the best because most of the time books cost money and they don't always have the biggest selection. Linda McMaken states that eBook downloads cost on average 99¢ to $9.99. Not all books are eBooks which is a downside for eBooks if people want a specific book that is not an eBook. According to Wikipedia, there are six million eBooks while there are about 130 million printed books according to Mashable. This is why libraries are extremely helpful.

Libraries are still very important in the Internet Era for many reasons such as providing education, information, individual improvement, and recreation that benefits people. Research has shown that libraries are more reliable and helpful because the library dates back further than what can be found online, it is more organized, and has information more readily available. Librarians are there to assist anyone who needs help, and the number of books is significantly greater than what can be found on the Internet. The library gives people a feeling of satisfaction in being able to feel the experience of reading or finding information. The Internet does not give individuals a confidence knowing the information they have found is correct and provides them something they can't personally experience. Sooner or later, with the Internet, people will run into situations where they are unable to find what they are looking for. On the other hand, libraries can help you find what you are looking for. The library offers books, newspaper articles, obituaries, and public records, which are reliable sources.

Works Cited

"Web History Timeline" by Pew Research http://www.pewinternet. org/2014/03/11/world-wide-web-timeline/ Web. October 28, 2018.

"11 Things You Pay For That Libraries Have For Free" https://www. investopedia.com/financial-edge/0611/13-things-you-pay-for-that-your-library-has-for-free.aspx Web. October 28, 2018.

"Google: There Are 129,864,880 Books in the Entire World" by Mashable https://mashable.com/2010/08/05/number-of-books-in-the-world/#7iiMoWSv5mqf Web. October 28, 2018.
"E-book" https://en.wikipedia.org/wiki/E-book Web. October 28, 2018.

"How do I get a library card? How much do they cost?" http://mtb.custhelp. com/app/answers/detail/a_id/44/~/how-do-i-get-a-library-card%3F-how-much-do-they-cost%3F Web. October 28, 2018.

"Internet usage in the United States- Statistics & Facts" by Statista https:// www.statista.com/topics/2237/internet-usage-in-the-united-states/ Web. October 24, 2018.

Radcliffe, Joyce B. "Library vs. Internet - Ten Good Reasons to Use the Library." www.tnstate.edu/library/publicservices/library_vs_internet. aspx. Web. 24 October 2018.

"Public Libraries" https://publiclibraries.com/ Web. October 19, 2018.

www.ingramcontent.com/pod-product-compliance
Lightning Source LLC
Chambersburg PA
CBHW030557130626
46552CB00006B/2582